Four Tales of Adventure

KLICKITAT – AND OTHER STORIES

MARK JENKINS

Mark Jenkins

**KLICKITAT — And Other Stories
(K.A.O.S.)**

ISBN 978-1-7352061-2-7

Connect with Mark:
markjenkinsbooks.com
www.facebook.com/markjenkins.MD
Twitter @MarkJenkinsMD1

Help fuel further adventures by going to my website and signing up for my periodic newsletter, where I'll share updates, backstory, tidbits, and more.

The delicious cover art was brilliantly crafted by
©Mars Dorian
www.marsdorian.com

I want to acknowledge all the great mentors I have learned from, and the great mentors I have yet to learn from. I would like to thank my family and friends who have put up with me all these years, and never failed to laugh at a stale pun (well, maybe a few times) but were also always there to listen. I especially want to thank my wife, Joanna, for her sense of humor, love and compassion.

This collection is dedicated to the memory of my father, Michael.

K.A.O.S. Four tales of adventure.

Heavywater. (© 2020: Original to this series) Vulcanologist Archimedes Jackson falls while solo climbing in Alaska and is rendered unconscious. Waking, he finds himself in unfamiliar territory and encounters a secretive band of armed men. Archimedes must discover their true intention if he's to survive and find his way home.

Klickitat. (© 2020: Original to this series) Gianna and her husband Esmond discover a strange circle of animal bones while climbing a remote route on Mount Adams. The higher they climb the more evidence they find that something deep in the dormant stratovolcano is wakening.

Protectors. (© 2020 - June) Takeo Kita embarks on a solo mountaineering trip in the rugged Olympic Mountains of Washington State. At the site of a tragic plane crash from decades earlier, he discovers a strange artifact, which propels him on a mythic action and adventure journey that alters the trajectory of his life and thousands of others.

Signals. (© 2020: Original to this series) Neurologist Alfred Osler is trapped in the isolated town of Whittier, Alaska when the only land access into town is unexpectedly closed. He befriends a deaf college student, Kalliope; and as a winter storm bears down, they discover they are the only people not mysteriously incapacitated as armed men lurk into town.

HEAVYWATER

"The Earth tells the truth"

Archimedes Jackson watched the slab of ice crash below, evaluated his predicament, and decided he was screwed.

Ten seconds ago, the 60-degree incline had been a solid, adherent snow-and-ice ramp over stone. But no longer. Now he hung from the tip of his left ice axe — supported by his left foot — hanging precariously above the glacier. Neither his right arm nor his right leg had any sort of anchoring contact with the mountain. He looked down and saw that the two crampon front-points on his left boot were dug solidly into the ice face.

He had selected this route to bypass the more difficult vertical ice spilling over the ridge to the east. It looked to be the safer route. And it was fine, until it wasn't.

His thoughts went back to the accident: his partner; falling.

Stop!

He gazed up and saw that only the tip of the pick was wedged into a tiny crack in the otherwise smooth rock; he was a hair's breadth from plummeting.

He needed firm support with his right arm and leg, so he searched for a way out of the quandary. But he was angled down and off to the right. He had lost his right ice axe: he hung sideways and down — dangling an arm and a leg like a kid hanging from a set of monkey-bars on a playground.

Attempting to swing his right leg to gain a foothold was out of the question, as it would likely pop the tip of the pick off its tiny sliver of a hold. His life depended upon that 2 mm of stainless steel staying hooked in the rock crack. If it came out, or the rock lip split, Archimedes would fall off the face. He held his breath. The roaring of water echoed from the glacier below.

His left leg began to fatigue and then cramp, but he couldn't risk shifting his weight much to relieve the tetany setting into the muscles. He panted short, calming breaths. The quadriceps in his left thigh began to quiver as the muscles exhausted their energy reserves. *Don't look down. Look up.*

He looked down, trying to see where he would fall. His quads began a clonic, Elvis-leg jerking; a sign of imminent muscle failure. A death dance.

He fell –

— and had a brief glimpse of the azure sky before his back slammed into the snow slope below, stunning him. Then he was in the air again, and felt a disorienting spin: the sky and the snow exchanged places before the glacier rose up and smacked him in the chest, driving the air from his lungs. A harsh rasping sound assaulted his ears and he recovered enough awareness to know he was sliding — and accelerating. Belly down, feet first, he struggled to drive the ice axe pick into the glacier to arrest the slide.

He saw the mountain face from which he'd just fallen retreat rapidly. Urgency and desperation gripped his brain as the primal centers screamed: he clawed with the axe and kicked with the crampons.

Stop. Please God. Stop!

A crampon front-point bit into the ice and drove his right knee up into his chest, somersaulting him backwards into the air. When he contacted the ice again, he was moving much faster and then began to tumble. Each jarring impact with the glacier punched him like a heavyweight boxer.

Shit.

Archimedes plunged into frigid water — and choked until he managed to get his face above the surface to gasp in a spluttering breath: he coughed. The nauseating sensation of falling continued to scream in his brain. He struggled in the torrent coursing rapidly downslope – a polished luge course of fast-moving ice-water.

Crap! I'm in a melt channel.

He felt ice grip his guts: he knew these rapid glacier-melt flows ultimately ended in a cliff or a crevasse. *I'm dead if I don't get out of this.*

He dug the pick of his axe into the closest edge of the channel, but the ice was too hard and he was moving too fast. The stream intersected with another and dumped Archimedes into a large basin, where crashing waves and swirling water pushed him under. Flailing up to the surface and gulping air, he saw that the strong currents were dragging him towards a swirling vortex at the opposite end of the basin. A huge drain hole, a moulin, was sucking the water hundreds of feet down into, and underneath, the glacier.

Death.

He fought in vain, but circled the drain; the moulin sucked him under. Struggling, he lost consciousness in the darkening, drowning-tunnel.

A concussive wave blasted through Archimedes and jarred him awake. He was underwater. Desperately kicking upwards, lungs screaming for air, he burst through the surface, and heaved and choked in the dark.

The warm water pushed him gently downstream. *Where the hell am I? What happened?*

His brain replayed everything as he tried to understand why he was still alive. Or perhaps he wasn't, and these were the last moments of an anoxic, dying brain, imagining a miraculous rescue in warm water, beaches, white sand, sun, and drinks with little umbrellas. *Maybe my brain is supplying me with soothing images as my neurons die. Bye-bye.*

Except there was no sun or sand, only darkness, as he floated along in the warm water.

He tried to concentrate on one thing. Just one thing. But his thoughts flitted and could not perch.

Nothing equated with any previous experience. The lukewarm water was soothing after the frigid cold but it didn't make sense. Nothing made sense.

Archimedes retrieved his headlight from his jacket pocket and switched it on. The beam bounced off walls and ceiling, which looked like the surface of a golf ball, with scalloped and concave chunks in the white ice. It was a cathedral-sized ice cavern that looked like someone had been at it with a large melon-baller. The ice facets reflected the LED light in jumping, ephemeral patterns.

More water channels poured in from the ice ceiling above.

Why is the water warm? Geothermal?

His awakening brain continued to pepper him with questions that he couldn't answer, and then settled on one: *Am I alive?*

That got his attention.

Well, if I'm not, then nothing matters. But if I am, then I need to stop pondering and focus on survival.

The trapped air in Archimedes' watertight pack kept him from sinking as he floated downstream. The dimpled ceiling began to glow, then ahead of him a bright spot appeared intermittently. The ice ceiling brightened into a powder-blue luminescence. The light downstream grew into a wide mouth: the exit.

He floated beyond the threshold and emerged underneath an overcast sky. The current slowed and flattened out into a shallow, muddy delta with a small channel in the center. His butt scraped the bottom and he rolled over onto his knees. Standing, he staggered to shore, collapsed onto all fours, retched, and blacked out.

Shivering woke him. He opened his eyes. Lying on his side, the view of the trees, mountains, and sky did not look right.

He sat up stiffly and rubbed his sore back. Fishing out his smartphone, he undid the protective case and thumbed the power button. His teeth chattered as the phone ran through its boot-up routine, stalled — and crashed. His hands shook as he tried it again. This time it complied, and glowed a happy welcome screen. It then flashed a big, colorful box, thanking him for his purchase. He clicked OK and then the phone fired off a bunch of prompts that he clicked through rapidly, with mounting frustration: *What language do you prefer? Please indicate your time zone. Would you like to hook up to your home network now? Any contacts to important?*

Fuck it.

The shivering intensified and he put the phone in his pocket to avoid dropping it. He sloshed back to just inside the cave mouth, where the air and water were warmer. He looked at his phone again and experienced a déjà-vu flashback to when he first got it. Blank. It was empty of all data, photos, everything — all blank. The apps were still there, though, and he pulled up the GPS map. It didn't need a cell tower or a WiFi connection. He hadn't expected a cell signal out in the Alaskan wilderness — and indeed, hadn't had one in days — but the GPS chip read satellite data.

Staring at his phone, shivers abating, he pleaded with it to find satellites. He had been using the smartphone GPS app for navigation for a few years now. It worked well, and he could forgo the extra weight of a separate electronic device, plus batteries. Once everything loaded up and the phone pinged the satellites, he should be able to see where the hell he was.

Standing knee-deep in the warm water, Archimedes looked up as the setting sun found a break in the clouds. In the distance were mountains and a fjord. *What the fuck?* Central Alaska had no fjords. It was more than a hundred miles from any ocean.

He looked at the smartphone.

No cell. *Expected.*

No GPS. *Why?*

Feeling his chest tighten and his heart hammer, Archimedes paused to use a breathing technique to counteract the rising adrenalin. After about thirty seconds he felt centered and calm enough to return his attention to the conundrum.

OK. I fell and got sucked down a moulin. I don't know where I am. I have no GPS signal and no clue where to go.

Pulling his mind away from the big-picture questions that thwarted him, he focused on his next immediate survival steps: gear check, and a fire. He took inventory of the gear he still had with him: pack, helmet, clothes, one ice axe, boots, crampons. He opened the pack and was relieved to find that the waterproof design had kept the contents dry. He pawed around inside, careful not to pull anything out lest he drop it into the water. He still had his emergency kit, dry socks, another base-layer, a waterproof journal, some food, a royal-blue Merino-wool sweater, a foldout multi-tool, a red goose-down parka, 100 meters of purple climbing rope, his fluorescent orange emergency satellite beacon, and a full 1-liter water bottle.

His shivering had stopped so he sloshed back out of the cave. He found higher ground to the left, out of the mud, at the tree line. *OK. Get a fire going. Turn on the emergency beacon and hit the SOS button.*

Archimedes dumped his pack on a cluster of rocks under a tall evergreen tree and pulled on the parka to ward off the cold. He pulled out the watertight bag containing the emergency kit. Inside were Band-Aids, a quick-clot bandage, a gauze roll, duct-tape, cloth tape, ibuprofen, waterproof matches, and a small hand-held bandsaw. He extracted the latter two items and then turned to search for wood.

The act of hunting around for fuel warmed his body. Most of the small limbs and sticks he gathered were wet but there were a few that were almost dry. He soon had enough, and made a small circle of stones, within which he staged the fuel. He tore a few pages out of his waterproof journal to make a central core, surrounded it with the driest twigs, and then added larger sticks.

He lit a match and eased it into the center, where the paper caught. He added a few more of the not-quite-so-damp twigs, and the small fire grew. Turning his attention to the emergency beacon, he pressed the *ON* button. When powered up, it would search for GPS-satellites and, once connected, the LED labelled *Signal* would glow green. He nursed the fire until he was certain it wouldn't immediately go out, and then hunted for more fuel.

Returning, he checked the beacon and was surprised to still see a red LED: no connection. Despite it not having yet contacted any satellites, he decided to activate the emergency signal anyway. He slid the cover off the SOS switch and pressed the red button, holding it until the LED flashed rapidly, indicating it was sending out a call for the cavalry. He hoped they were listening.

Archimedes turned his attention back to the fire, and another thirty minutes of tending yielded a good blaze. Hunger gnawed at him; he broke off a piece of an energy bar. He chewed the cinnamon-raisin morsel slowly and put a large stick onto the crackling fire. The wood smoke stung his eyes and he blinked away tears.

He paced back to the woods to gather more fuel. He returned, squatted on his haunches, fed the fire, and tried to come to grips with his growing fear. *Where are the satellites?* He'd been in some forsaken places before and had lost sat signal, but never for this long. It didn't feel right. Was there some sort of sustained electromagnetic interference in the atmosphere? Massive solar flares? Nuclear war?

Stop the hysterics: keep your wits, he chided himself. *It's probably just local terrain blocking signal reception from a satellite low on the horizon.* He should try a different location for the beacon, after he had warmed up and dried out. He had about two hours of daylight left, and so he could walk a little further downstream to find an open spot and set the unit there.

"Hands up! Move and you're dead," came a sharp call from behind him.

Still squatting on his haunches, he raised both hands in the air, feeling like a bandit caught red-handed. He heard jogging footfalls, and then a man dressed all in black appeared in front of Archimedes and pointed a rifle at his chest.

"Sprechen Sie Deutsch?"

"No. English," said Archimedes.

"Lie flat on the ground, arms out. Don't look at me." He had a British accent. Archimedes complied with the order.

"Check him for weapons," said another voice in a thick Scottish brogue. "And search his kit."

"Aye, sir."

Archimedes felt the back of his jacket being lifted and a pair of hands pawed his armpits, chest, lower back, belt, and buttocks in turn. His knife was pulled out of its sheath on his belt. He heard fabric rustling and the muffled plops of falling objects. Then a gasp. "Cor blimey, sir. Look at this."

Archimedes heard boot-falls, and then a muttered curse. The air was pierced by metallic snicks and he pictured the bolt on the rifle.

"Don't shoot me," he said.

"Furry-boots ye fae, Yank?" asked the Scotsman.

"What?"

"He said, whereabouts are you from, Yankee?" translated the man with the rifle.

"Anchorage."

"We should do' im. I'm tinkin' he's a Gerry," said another voice, with another accent. Irish?

"Look, guys. I've had a really shitty day. I fell off a fucking mountain and went down a Goddamned moulin," said Archimedes. "Can you just take whatever you want, point me in the direction of the nearest town, and leave me alone?"

"He's no Gerry. Look at that purple rope, red anorak, blue jumper... and what the bloody hell is that blinkin' thing?"

"Look. I'm unarmed," said Archimedes, his voice rising in pitch.

"Except the knife, ye wanker."

"Except the knife," acknowledged Archimedes.

"What's te blinky ting?" asked the Irishman.

"I can explain if you would just give me the chance. Can I sit up to talk with you?"

Pause.

Archimedes assumed that a series of head nods, raised eyebrows, and/or throat-slicing gestures were being exchanged by the men behind him, deciding his fate. His saliva turned to dust as he waited for a reply.

"Aye. Sit up slowly, lad. Hands where we can see 'em."

Archimedes trembled as he sat up painfully. He looked around — and then blurted out, "Holy shit!"

He surveyed — and then resurveyed — the bunch in front of him. Naturally, the weapons attracted his eyes first: Thompson sub-machine guns; Colt-45 semi-auto pistols; a bolt action rifle with a scope; and a few stubby-looking guns with the magazines sticking out of the side. The muzzles, more or less pointed in his direction, projected from a loose semi-circle of eight men facing him. They were dressed in all black; black fatigues, black wool caps, with blacking smudged all over their faces.

Archimedes' mind felt numb as he tried to decipher the image in front of him. For their part, the men were studying Archimedes with the same frozen facial expressions that he must be displaying. Plumes of exhaled air condensed into clouds in the waning light.

"Come wi' me, lad," said the Scotsman, and beckoned with his hand.

Archimedes walked after the big man. From behind him, he heard a hushed exchange.

"I still say he's a Gerry."

"Gerries don't prance around with purple ropes, red jackets, and red puttees, ya twit."

"Pooftah?"

"Why would dere be a pooftah, here in te middle o' nowhere?"

"Daft?"

"Possibly."

And then they were out of earshot. The Scotsman stopped and Archimedes noted that one of the men with a Thompson had followed them. He forced himself to slow his breathing. *Is this some sort of hazing ritual? A battle reenactment? Yes, that has to be it. Some sort of World War Two role-playing thing, and these people are really into it. Deeply.*

The Scotsman pointed to a log and said, "Have a sit." Archimedes sat, and looked at him and the guy with the sub-machine gun, standing six feet away.

"You'd best answer truthfully," said the British guy with the Thompson.

Archimedes stared at him for a moment and then nodded.

"What're you doing here?" asked the Scot.

"I wish I knew," said Archimedes. "I was climbing a mountain and then I fell into a stream and got swept under the glacier and came out of that tunnel over there." He pointed to the cave mouth.

"What's your name?" demanded the Scot.

"Archimedes Jackson."

"Definitely a Yank," said the Brit, and then was hushed into silence by a glare from the bushy-eyebrowed Scotsman.

"Tell me about your kit. And what the blazes is this?" demanded the Scot, holding out the beacon.

"It's an emergency beacon."

"How's it work? Who are ye signaling?"

Archimedes explained the mechanics of the device, including the types of satellites it connected with. He could see the signal-strength LED, which was still red. The other LED, the SOS one, blipped three short, followed by three long, red flashes.

"I can see the Morse code S-O-S, but how the hell is anyone supposed to see that from more than a few yards away? Bloody useless."

Archimedes explained again about GPS satellites.

The Scot muttered something with a rolling *r-r-r-r* sound and spat on the ground.

Archimedes wasn't sure whether he was speaking or gargling loose a clump of phlegm but decided to err on the side of caution. "I beg your pardon?"

"He said, you're speaking rubbish," said the Brit.

"Aye! We got nay time for games. Yer comin' with us until we figure out what to do with you," announced the Scot, and then turned to the group. "Lads, be ready to move agin with'n the hour."

There was a muted chorus of, "Aye, sir."

They doused the fire, and along with it Archimedes' hopes of being left alone. The men checked their khaki rucksacks and prepared to leave. Miserably, Archimedes repacked his upended gear, under the watchful eye of Tommy-gun, who'd been functioning as a translator for the Scot. The Brit looked closely at the crampons that Archimedes was securing to the outside of his pack.

"Ain't seen crampons like those before. Nor the ice axe," he said.

"Petzl, a French company, makes them," said Archimedes.

The Brit scrunched his eyes. "Sounds German."

"Yes. I guess it does," said Archimedes, and shrugged. "Do you climb?"

"Oh yes!" said Tommy-gun, visibly straightening. "Learnt everything from my dad, who was on the Mount Everest expedition in '24. Proper heroes, they were. You know it's been – what? – almost twenty years, and my dad still talks about it. He reckons they made it to the summit, George Mallory and young Sandy Irvine, and then fell on the way down."

Archimedes stiffened and stopped stuffing his pack. He looked down to see that his hands were shaking. *Did he just say that '24 was almost twenty years ago?*

"Maybe when the war's over I can join the next expedition," said Tommy-gun. "I'll carry the Union Jack up there and maybe I'll find there's already one atop. There's some strong, fit lads in the Alpine Club as well as some old rich gaffers who's done some first ascents back in the day. I'll climb with whoever's good and I'll not look sideways at the sterling, if you follow me. I just want my chance. Hey, you alright?"

"Just lightheaded," said Archimedes. "I think... I need to eat something."

"Here, have a *tooth duller*," said Tommy-gun. He took from his jacket pocket and offered a brownish, flat rectangle. He beamed a smile that was missing an incisor. "Biscuits. Go on, you'll get used to 'em."

Archimedes took it and hesitantly nibbled its corner. He managed to bite off a piece without fracturing a tooth and began to grind away at the tasteless, unsalted hardtack.

The Brit laughed at him. "Not as good as Yank rations, I bet."

"Umm… yeah," said Archimedes. His mind was still wrestling with the anachronistic conversation, clothing and weapons. *If it is a reenactment group, they're damn good.* But unease threatened his composure: *What if it's real?*

"My name's Wylie," said Tommy-gun, and offered his hand, which Archimedes accepted and shook. The Scot approached them, carrying something in his arms. He handed Archimedes the emergency beacon with a sharp look, and then pivoted to give the ice axe and knife to Wylie, who slung his sub-machine gun over his shoulder to accept the tools. Archimedes detected a faint whiff of pipe tobacco as the Scot strode off.

Wylie shrugged and inspected the axe: he turned it over in his hands to peer at the spike, adze and pick; hefted it; and swung it through the air a few times. His eyebrows rose up his forehead and then he masked his face and turned to his rucksack, where he began attaching the axe — shooting occasional side glances at Archimedes.

Archimedes sensed something familiar in the boyish, gap-toothed smile. *He's so young — a teenager: I wonder if he always talks so much.*

Archimedes finished stuffing his pack, then looked around at the men strapping on skis and snowshoes, and felt another wave of unease. He'd seen wooden skis with flat metal plates and leather straps before — and wooden snowshoes with woven rattan and wicker — but only in museums, or up on the walls of a ski lodge with signs reading *Do Not Touch*. As he looked around at various pieces of gear that the men were packing or equipping, his gaze rested on the figure of a tall thin man leaning on a wooden-shafted ice axe. Embers glowed in the bowl of the pipe pressed to his lips; his dark eyes watched Archimedes.

They headed out on snowshoes and skis. Archimedes matched their pace but kept breaking through the crust, creating calf-deep postholes in the snow and more work for his tired body. He was fourth in line and closely flanked by Wylie. He listened to the men talk. Some had Scandinavian accents and there were a variety of UK accents, and it was clear that the Scot was in charge. *But who are these people and where are they going?*

After several hours of trudging along in a narrow valley under the glow of a half-moon and thin cirrus clouds, the

Scotsman ordered a halt near a sheer rock wall where a deep natural crack barricaded by a clump of large boulders offered concealment. Most of the men plunked their rucksacks down in the snow against the house-sized rocks, but the Scotsman had a quick conversation with one of the men on skis, who then turned and continued uphill in the valley. Archimedes heard the *whisk-whisk* of his skis as he disappeared into the night — and then he removed his pack to find a spot to rest.

Most of the men had distributed themselves in a loose circle within the crack, huddled in groups of two or three, against the cold. Wylie and the Scot were outside the ring of boulders, and appeared deep in conversation.

"What do ya do in America, Yank?" asked one of the men.

"I'm a geologist. Vulcanologist, actually," answered Archimedes. There was no immediate reply. The men slowly chewing rations with blank expressions looked like a ring of cows chewing the cud.

"A what?"

"A vulcanologist. I study volcanoes."

"Why would you want to do that?"

"To understand them better and to help predict when they might erupt."

The fact that not one of the men uttered a joke about Mr. Spock or Star Trek spoke volumes. Archimedes had never met anyone who didn't whip out that tired old pun when informed of his occupation. In any event, they seemed more interested in food than further inquiries and returned to eating in silence.

Wylie — who seemed to be Archimedes' appointed guardian/interrogator — approached, plopped his rucksack down, and sat on it. He rustled around in his jacket and produced another tooth-breaker — or molar-grinder, or whatever the dental-damaging biscuits were called — and offered it. Archimedes shook his head. The Brit broke off a piece and crunched on it noisily. He removed Archimedes' ice axe from its lashings on his rucksack and brought it close to his own face to peer at it. After a while he held it out and said, "So, Archimedes where do you climb with such a short, light axe?"

Archimedes paused for a moment to consider the layers in the inquiry. He'd seen the waist-high axe that the tall man with the pipe carried and knew that axes had historically gotten quite a lot shorter: in less than a hundred years they'd gone from heavy, six-foot-tall wooden poles shod with iron, to lightweight, knee-high, gently curved aluminum tubes affixed with stainless-steel tools. He decided the question was likely honest curiosity mixed with some disbelief in the functionality of the axe, and a bit of skepticism that Archimedes was a mountaineer.

"Alaska mostly, but also the volcanoes in the Cascades. That axe really shines in steep snow and ice," said Archimedes.

"Have you climbed McKinley?"

"Yes."

"That's a rough one, I hear. Big expedition climbing," said Wylie. "Back home it's Ben Nevis and Snowdonia for me and, across the channel, I fancy Chamonix and Zermatt. At least I did before the Nazis buggered it all up. They shut everyone out so they could get some first ascents for their bloody Reich. Can't believe those damned warring ironmongers Heckmair and Vörg conquered the Eiger-Nordwand. Bloody deathtrap, that is. Made it out of the White Spider in a storm by the skin of their teeth, I read. Probably hammered so many bloody pitons into the rock that you can walk up it like an iron staircase now."

During the turn of the topic towards the Alps, Wylie's voice had risen in volume, and he punctuated some of his words with stabs of the axe pick into the snow between his legs.

For the most part, Archimedes listened in silence, issuing an occasional nod or monosyllabic agreement. That first ascent of that infamous north face was in 1938, he recalled, and before that there had been so many climbers' bodies piling up below that the Swiss had banned attempts for a number of years, and everyone had considered it unclimbable. *Wylie is genuinely heated about it, though — a fresh wound.*

"So, what's it made of?" asked Wylie, gesturing the spike at Archimedes. "Aluminium?"

"I'm sorry. What?"

"Your axe shaft is aluminium, I reckon — like on aircraft, like the Spitfires. Light and strong. Is it a prototype?" asked Wylie, the words tumbling out. Then he paused. "Say... are you one of the Yank blokes from that new Alpine division? I

26

hear they're working on some new gear. You know, my dad said that Wallisch Täsch — who designed the axes for the '24 expedition — said that lighter and smaller is the future for alpinism. That is spot on, I think."

Thirty-thousand feet above them, a gap appeared in the thinning cirrus clouds; the moonlight intensified, casting sharp shadows on the snow. Wylie was still talking about *the new alpinism* and gesticulating with Archimedes' ice axe to emphasize his points. Archimedes nodded in what he hoped were the right places, but his attention had snapped to the rock wall where the moonlight struck. He stood and took a step towards it — and his pulse quickened. In another step, a pattern emerged, and he could barely restrain the urge to shout.

He leaned close to inspect the wall, and smiled at the whorls of light beige wedges adrift in the dark tan, igneous rock. He removed his right glove and touched it with his fingers and then he was certain: *rhomb-porphyry*. A rare and beautiful discovery — from the end of the Carboniferous period extending into the Permian: over 200 million years ago.

Then his heart sank. He knew a specimen like this had only been discovered in three places: Antarctica, the East African Rift Valley, and the Oslo Rift. He was certain he could cross the first two off the list: *How the hell am I in Norway?*

"You alright?"

"Umm… yes," he stuttered. "It's a… uh… rare type of rock."

"Will it help us win the war?"

"What?"

"I said, will it help us beat the Nazis?"

"Uh... no."

"Not much use then, is it?"

Archimedes' fingers numbed painfully as the cold slab sucked away his body heat. His mind drifted to Alaska and his cabin in the woods. He ought to be there, by the fire, alone. Not here. Not Norway. A shiver coursed through him and he pulled his hand away. He looked again at the rhomb-porphyry and imagined reality shattering like a delicate crystal under a clumsily wielded geologist's hammer.

Christ! This shit's real: Norway; UK and Norwegian commandos; in the 1940s.

"Let's move it, lads," ordered the Scotsman. And just like that, they were trudging on again. Wylie started off next to Archimedes and then stopped off to the side. Archimedes halted and turned but the man immediately behind him grunted and pointed ahead. "Go," he said.

Archimedes resumed his plodding, grateful that the depth of the snow was shallower then earlier. They were still headed uphill and he could see that the terrain had become more jagged with the elevation. Tall conifers cast elongated Christmas-tree shadows as the moon sank towards the horizon. As his eyes took in the topography, his brain grappled with explanations for *how* he could possibly be in Norway in the 1940s — clearly smack in the middle of World War Two — but found only cold, featureless, impenetrable stone for answers. There was no rational explanation, yet here he was.

He glanced over his shoulder at the men behind him, and spotted Wylie next to the Scotsman. They appeared deep in conversation but then the Scotsman suddenly looked up, making eye contact. Archimedes held the stare for a second or two and then turned and caught up with the man in front, but not before receiving a poke from behind.

About two hours later, the Scot called a halt near a stream. Rucksacks were dropped and canteens were filled. Wylie and the Scotsman came over to stand with Archimedes.

"Lance Corporal Wylie here thinks you might be part of a Yank mountaineering division. Is that true?" asked the Scot.

"Not exactly."

"Bloody hell! Why can't you Yanks just answer honestly!"

"Well, look ... I'm separated from my group because I fell. They're just surveying, gathering intelligence. They have no plan for any activity in the area, and they won't search for me out here. I'm on my own now," said Archimedes, hoping his half-truths would pass muster, although he was pretty certain about the last two points.

From beneath bushy brows, the Scotsman's dark eyes penetrated Archimedes like a core sampler. Archimedes did not break eye contact but focused on keeping his expression composed. The Scotsman's head nodded almost imperceptibly and then he said, "Wylie says you could be an asset and help us."

Archimedes smiled. "Yes."

"But I dunno if I can trust ye," said the Scot. "Aye, the Yanks are with us in this war, but how do I know yer not a spy? You've got some bloody queer gear, and you talk nonsense about space beams. We're meeting some locals and then we'll decide what to do wi' ye."

Without waiting for an answer, the Scot moved on and roused the group into motion again.

Wylie paced along next to Archimedes. After a few minutes he said, "Don't mind the commander. I trust ya."

"Thanks. You too, bro."

"Beg your pardon?"

"I mean, you're a good man, Wylie. I trust you, too." *But your trust in me is probably misplaced.*

They plodded along in silence, following a set of ski tracks. The trail curved and the dense trees began to thin. As they approached the edge of a glade, the group suddenly stopped and split to hide in the trees on either of the trail. Wylie unslung his Thompson and crouched down in the snow. Archimedes followed his lead, but noted that he lacked any way to defend himself. He started to ask what was going on, but Wylie put an index finger to his lips and stared ahead.

From across the glade, Archimedes heard the whisper of cross-country skis a moment before a man appeared. It was the point-man who'd been sent off earlier by the Scotsman.

The group stood and closed to form a circle off to one side of the trail, with the Scotsman and the point-man in the center. Wylie and Archimedes joined them.

"Any sign of Grouse?" asked the Scot.

"There's a shelter hut up ahead. Smoke's coming out the chimney. Skis outside," answered the point-man.

"Gerries?"

"No, sir. Too far from the garrison."

On the horizon, above a range of mountains, a pre-dawn glow painted the clouds pink. Archimedes slowly reached his right hand into a pocket inside his parka, feeling for his smartphone. He kept his eyes on the Scotsman as he thumbed it on. Keeping it hidden in his coat, he glanced down at the screen so the glow wouldn't attract stares. Still no GPS. And no cell service. It was a futile attempt to deny the truth, he knew, but he couldn't quash the longing for home.

Archimedes stashed the phone and looked up to see several heads bent over a cloth map, studying it with a flashlight the size of a toaster, which produced a feeble flax-yellow light and looked like it weighed a lot: the small Irish guy they called Mickey had to use both arms to keep it pointed at the map. The anemic light winked off, then on, then dimmed, and finally cut out completely. The Scotsman swore.

"Batteries, sir," explained the Irishman.

"Do I look like I just came off the banana boat?" hissed the Scot.

"No, sir."

"Perhaps I can help," said Archimedes, stepping towards them with his headlight, a pigeon-egg-sized blue box attached to a stretchy yellow headband. When he got close to them, he flicked the headlamp on, at the lowest setting, and they jumped back at the pure white brightness.

"What the blazes?" exclaimed Point-man.

Archimedes showed it to them and pointed the light at the map. He was scolded for looking at it, so he handed the light over and diverted his gaze as they studied it. He stole glances, and saw Point-man get out an old-school compass — and then argue with the Scot about where they were and whether the cabin ahead was the correct rendezvous point.

They finally came to a resolution, and the Scotsman gave the order for the group to move again.

An hour later, they approached the cabin. Wood smoke rose from the chimney and the snow blanketed all sounds. Weapons were unslung and pointed at the ground. They walked as if this was a casual dinner meeting at the snow lodge after a day of skiing and they were ready for a snifter of brandy, a pipe, and some good cheer. Except Archimedes could feel the tension. It brought to mind the time he wound a new G-string too tightly on his guitar, which twanged and ruptured on the first chord.

Two men appeared from the shadows of the cabin, one on each side, rifles raised. Archimedes watched their exchange with the Scotsman. Some signal satisfied, the groups relaxed. Two additional men came out of the cabin and everyone exchanged handshakes and smiles. Most went into the cabin with the Scotsman. Two remained outside on guard duty with Archimedes.

Now that he was no longer generating heat from moving uphill, cold penetrated Archimedes' bones. He stomped in place to warm up, then gave up and rooted around in his pack for his red parka. He pulled it out, donned it, and zipped it up, watched by two sets of cold eyes. The cabin door opened, spilling warm yellow light onto the hoar frost coating the snow drifts. Two men he had not previously seen came out; the two that had been standing outside quickly went inside.

Hunger gnawed at Archimedes' belly, and his thoughts turned inward. When he was moving with the commandos he had something to focus on, but waiting around like this brought emptiness.

Visceral sensations of cold, travel, and hunger collided with the impossibilities of time and place, yielding disorientation. He felt as upended as when the commandos had dumped all his gear out in the snow. He still didn't know exactly what the group was planning and, more importantly, he had no idea how to get back to his own time — or if that was even possible.

Uncertainty threatened to dump him into despair; he slowed his breathing. *Focus on what you know.*

He was being dragged along by a small commando band of twelve, who were from the UK and Norway and paranoid about being caught. Obviously, they were in Norway and in an area with a strong German presence.

They're not here for tea. But what are they after?

He scoured his memory for any information about what happened in Scandinavia during World War Two: Finland had joined the Axis, largely due to their hatred of the Soviets, with whom they were already at war; Norway had been invaded by Germany; and Sweden had stayed neutral. Archimedes only knew that it was the early 1940s and that it was winter. He didn't want to spook the commandos by asking for specific details. He wasn't sure it would help all that much anyway, since he lacked detailed knowledge of the time period. *I'll just have to stick to my principles and wing it.*

A memory floated to the surface. UK raiders had ceaselessly driven daggers into the Nazi machine throughout the war by sneaking in and blowing shit up: U-boat bases, secret weapons facilities, and research labs. The force he was with seemed too small to have the scale-up potential to attack a base, so that left... what? *Are they meeting up with a larger force? What did Norway have? Damnit, I should know this.*

"Mate, you're wanted inside," said Wylie. Archimedes hadn't heard him approach. The look on Wylie's face suggested it wasn't an invitation. Dawn broke on the horizon.

As Archimedes crossed the threshold of the cabin he felt warmth on his face. Wood smoke, kerosene, and pipe tobacco penetrated his nostrils, and then he noted another odor: cooked food. When his eyes adjusted to the dim light, he saw over half a dozen men, standing and sitting around a table in the main room, studying him. Animal hides covered the wooden floor, and through a doorway he saw another group of men hunched over a table ravenously spooning something from bowls into their mouths. His stomach growled.

Wylie pointed to an empty chair at the main table and Archimedes sat down. Wylie disappeared into the back room. From directly across the table, the Scotsman introduced him as, "Archimedes, the lost Yank straggler we picked up."

This earned the Scot harsh stares from two of the men that had been waiting for them at the cabin. There was a quick exchange in a language that Archimedes assumed was Norwegian. He couldn't understand their words, but their facial expressions and body language made their meaning clear: *Why didn't you just put a bullet in the back of his head and dump him in a fjord?*

Wylie came back into the main room with a steaming bowl and approached the table. It killed the conversation. The Norwegians stared at the center of the table. The Scotsman watched Wylie. Archimedes studied them all. One of the Norwegians had wavy black hair, strong cheekbones, and prominent, arched eyebrows that made him look as though he was surprised — when he wasn't frowning. The other one had close-cropped blonde hair and large canine teeth. Wylie put the bowl in front of Archimedes, making eye contact. He gestured at the animal hides on the floor and then at the bowl and said, "Reindeer stew. Bloody delicious!"

Archimedes peered at the stew in front of him, and saliva bathed his mouth at the aroma. He nodded his thanks and looked across at Scotsman and the Norwegians, who appeared content to let him eat. He hefted a spoonful into his mouth, and the savory taste of potatoes, turnips, and venison overruled any concern about the men in front of him. After shoveling in several more mouthfuls, he paused and said, "Thank you. I'm grateful for this food."

He slurped down the rest of the stew and then searched in his pack. After a moment, he found what he was looking for, and extracted a large chocolate bar. He unwrapped one end and broke off a square, which he popped in his mouth. Then he handed the bar over to a still scowling Norwegian, who seemed surprised but accepted and cautiously sniffed it, before breaking off a square. He handed it over to the Scot. Archimedes watched their expressions as the bar was passed around the table, and squares disappeared into mouths.

"That's very good chocolate," said the Norwegian with the black-wavy hair. "We don't have these luxuries. Most people are starving." The blonde Norwegian grunted in agreement.

"Thanks for sharing, lad," said the Scotsman. He stood and turned to face the other room. In a raised voice, he said, "Time for sleep. Pair up for watch duty for two-hour shifts."

"Aye, sir," echoed around the cabin. Outside, the weak winter morning light barely penetrated the thin curtains covering the windows.

There were three cots, all low to the floor, and all occupied. Archimedes assumed these were for the men of higher ranks; certainly not for him. Wylie showed Archimedes a spot in the corner where he could bed down on a reindeer hide. *Perhaps Prancer or Dasher should have been faster.* He arranged his pack as a pillow and laid his parka over him as a blanket. Cold air blew through gaps between the logs of the cabin's walls. He was so tired that even the unresolved question of what they were going to do with him couldn't halt his descent into a deep slumber. He dreamt of rock towers, water and automatic weapons.

It was dark when Archimedes woke. He got up slowly and stiffly, and went into the small kitchen where he was given a bowl of oatmeal and a cup of tea. Both were thin and watery but nourishing. Wylie, looking chipper, appeared by his side. "Commander wants to see ya," he said, pointing to the front door.

Outside, lit by the glow of a kerosene lantern, the Scotsman and the black-haired Norwegian were talking. They stopped abruptly as Archimedes approached.

"Hello, Archimedes," said the Norwegian. "My name is Torvald. You must forgive my manners yesterday. You were not expected." His English was perfectly enunciated and had a musical Scandinavian lilt.

"No worries."

Torvald cocked his head to one side and his eyebrows came together. Hastily, Archimedes added, "It's okay. I understand. Thank you for your hospitality."

Torvald nodded and his eyebrows relaxed. He said, "These are dangerous and dark times but we're all fighting together against the Nazis, yes."

It wasn't a question, but Archimedes nodded in agreement.

"An American here is very unusual but we are allies, yes," Torvald said, and then paused. "We do something... important. You will not be harmed but we cannot let you go until two days from now. You understand, yes?"

"I think so," said Archimedes. His heart rate rose as he thought through what he was about to say. "It's hydroelectric, isn't it? Your target is a dam."

Both men's eyes bulged.

"Who told you that?" demanded the Scotsman, as Torvald snarled and swore.

"No one," said Archimedes. "I recall from history... um... from the history of Norway before the war. Norway's very advanced in hydroelectric technology. The Nazis are using this and you want to stop them." Archimedes watched them carefully as he spoke. From their reactions, he was now certain. "I can help you," he added.

The Scotsman looked at Torvald and said, "Our climber, Wylie, says he knows his stuff. We could use him to help us scout. We've still not decided the route."

"I don't know," said Torvald, shaking his head. "I must confer with Stig."

He walked away.

"Well, you're knee deep in it now, lad."

"I guess I am," said Archimedes, and walked towards the cabin.

At the door, he paused and exhaled the breath he'd been holding. *Why can't I just be home? This can't be real.*

But it is what it is, isn't it? It's time to decide: crevasse of self-pity, or reality?

Archimedes stomped the snow off his boots and went inside. The cabin was rarely occupied by the full contingent: faces changed; men came and went. Currently, it was bustling with commandos opening, laying out, and cataloging the gear newly arrived from a large toboggan, which had been towed and pushed uphill to the cabin by three exhausted men on skis.

As the commandos worked, Archimedes heard exclamations ranging from excitement to disappointment. The commander and Torvald were circulating around, occasionally squatting to inspect gear, and chat. Faces smiled back.

Sometime long after midnight, Archimedes fell asleep in his spot on the floor. He got up at around noon and was told by Point-man that the commander wanted to see him. Outside he found the Scotsman, Torvald and the blonde Norwegian, who turned out to be Stig, standing under a tall evergreen tree.

"Well, we've thought through your offer," began the Scotsman, "and there's something you should know. This might be a one-way mission." He coughed and looked at Torvald before continuing. "You see, Hitler has ordered that all captured commandos are to be interrogated, then executed. It happened with the previous raid here, months ago. There's no prisoner-of-war status for us. And the Nazis will go into Norwegian villages and butcher people if they think any Norwegian has engaged in partisan acts. If they capture any of my lads — or you — they'll gut us, but they'll know it was an Allied commando raid. If they capture any local Norwegians actively engaged in the raid it will lead to the slaughter of Norwegian civilians. Let that sink into your head for a bit."

Archimedes understood. It had to be an "official" British raid. This explained the British uniforms they all wore underneath their winter clothes, including the Norwegians, who were now *de facto* British servicemen.

Wait, did he say there was a previous raid? This means the Germans already know the dam is a target and will most certainly be wise to further attempts. Have they thought this through? Why not go blow up a different dam?

Archimedes realized he was being studied by the three men, and broke off his thoughts.

"I can see the wheels turning in yer head," said the Scotsman. "Now you're beginnin' to understand."

"The good part is that if the Germans shoot or capture you, they will know you are American, yes," said Stig. "This is good for our people. Not so great for you."

"So if you still want to help, you will be allowed, but you must do exactly as we say," said Torvald, "and we won't think twice about leaving you."

"—or shooting you," added Stig. Torvald nodded his agreement.

"So, still game, lad?" asked the Scotsman.

"Yes," answered Archimedes. Penetrating cold bit, and he trembled.

"Good. We have some scouting for you and Wylie, then. Get your kit, meet me inside, you leave in an hour."

Archimedes' throat tightened. *Oh man, what have I gotten myself into?*

Inside the cabin, Archimedes sat down at the main table with Wylie, the Scotsman, Stig, Torvald, and two others.

The Scotsman unfolded a cloth map and pointed to their target. "We still need to determine the best route to the complex at Vemork. Intelligence has determined three options: circling around to the plateau above, then traveling down the hill along the penstocks that feed water to the generators, here; or scaling up the cliff, here; or crossing the suspension bridge, here." He tapped each location with the lip of his pipe, and looked around the table into each of our eyes.

"We need to know two things: recent German defensive placements, and whether the cliff is climbable. Our sources inside the dam have given us as much as they can on the Germans, but the information is more than two months old — and they risked all bloody hell to get it to us — and all we know about the cliff are from aerial photographs."

"The Germans are expecting an attack on the water pipes — the *penstocks*, as you call them — and have fortified the hill area with landmines, alarms, and electrified wires," said Torvald. "We shouldn't attack where they expect us to."

"If the suspension bridge is still unguarded, it will be our fastest way in," said Stig. "It is only wide enough for two men, long, and exposed, but if the Germans aren't watching it's the best route."

"I don't think aerial photographs can tell me whether a route is climbable," said Wylie. "I need to see the cliff."

"Exactly," said the Scot, "and that's what you and Archimedes just volunteered to do. You'll climb up the opposite side and look down on the cliff and the main hydroelectric buildings. Take as many notes as you can and report back."

"Aye, sir," said Wylie.

Archimedes nodded. He looked at the map again. They were raiding a complex of buildings, below and quite some distance from the actual dam, which was up on a plateau. A series of penstocks cascaded downhill, delivering pressurized water to the buildings that housed the turbine generators.

His thoughts drifted to the best way to accomplish the scouting mission and, without thinking, he extracted his smartphone and thumbed it on.

"What the bloody hell is that?" demanded the Scotsman.

Archimedes jumped. The Norwegians flinched and appeared particularly upset — which was conveyed by a baring of teeth and a partial unsheathing of knives. He had seen this twice now. It was as if he were a stray wolf meeting a new pack, and had committed a serious *faux pas*.

He told them that it was a kind of telephone that could take pictures. As he listened to himself, his own words sounded weird, particularly when he considered the types of telephones to which they were accustomed. *I probably sound completely crazy to them.*

"Oh, so you can call Uncle Adolf, you spy?" said Stig, showing his large canines.

Archimedes tried explaining the smartphone but then realized he was just digging a deeper hole, and opted to show them instead.

"Knock me over with a feather," exclaimed the Scot after Archimedes snapped a photo of the commander and showed it to him on the screen.

"But that is just a trick with mirrors. The gap across the gorge is two kilometers or more," said Torvald. "Your toy is useless."

By way of answer, Archimedes went outside, picked out a distant cliff, perhaps two miles away, and zoomed in with the camera app. He turned around to show the results to the men who had followed him out; mouths hung open and heads shook in disbelief.

"What about at dusk or night?"

"It's fine. If the plant is lit up I should be able to get some good photos," said Archimedes. The battery icon showed 25%; he thumbed the phone off quickly. *Come on, don't die on me.*

Back inside the cabin, he prepped with Wylie. They packed canteens and some of the biscuits (to keep dentists back home in business) and soon headed out.

Wylie broke trail and Archimedes followed. After an hour of travel through the woods Archimedes heard the sound of rushing water. Wylie stopped to check their bearings. "We need to keep the brook on our left as we gain altitude," he whispered.

Archimedes nodded. *This terrain is so beautiful.*

They continued on in silence, snow absorbing the crunch of their boots. Even though the sun was still above the horizon the weak light and the overcast skies made it seem like dusk. Wylie led them to a steep slope and began to zigzag up. As they moved higher, and the trees thinned and the roaring of the brook faded, Archimedes became aware of a humming sound. *Machinery.*

He stopped and turned to look for the source, and across a gorge saw a cliff face. On the top was collection of concrete buildings lit by flood flights, but his vantage point revealed only the upper floors. Wylie appeared next to him and whispered, "That's our target, but we'll need to get higher to be able to see down on it."

Wylie trudged further uphill and Archimedes lingered for a few more moments to gaze at the cliff. Despite the darkening sky he spotted small evergreen trees dotting the face. He turned and followed Wylie, who soon came to a halt under a rock band.

"Almost," said Wylie, as Archimedes caught up to him. "Let's find a way up this wall."

Archimedes moved south along the band and Wylie moved north; both searched for a route up.

Archimedes stopped at a fissure that was a yard in width, and looked to run up the full height of the band – perhaps twenty feet. *This chute is almost vertical, but it looks ice free.*

He called softly to Wiley, who came over to look. "Look's good, mate," said Wiley after inspecting it. "After you."

Archimedes ascended the fissure and emerged at the top, and looked across the gorge at their target. *I think this is high enough.* Wylie scrambled up, sat beside him, and pulled out a pair of binoculars. "Aye, this is good," he said as he scanned through the lenses.

Archimedes got his phone to begin taking photos. The biting cold rapidly numbed his fingers as he manipulated the camera app to zoom in on different aspects of the defenses at Wylie's directions.

"Bastards!" said Wylie. *"Hitler's buzzsaw,* at the far end of the bridge."

"What's that?"

Wylie looked at him for a few seconds with an expression that was difficult to read. "MG-42 heavy machine gun; very high rate of fire. I guess you Yanks haven't seen it in action yet — and you don't want to. Cut you right in half."

Archimedes nodded slowly, and Wylie returned to his scrutiny. *I wonder how long he's been a commando. He's so young but there's a hard edge of experience.*

"Guard change," whispered Wylie, and looked at his watch.

Archimedes' fingers had progressed beyond numbness and felt like they were being slowly crushed with pliers of frozen steel. It was becoming harder to hold and use the phone, and then his breath caught. The battery icon was flashing red: <10%.

Oh shit!

He quickly thumbed it off, unzipped his parka, and snuggled the phone into the base layers of his clothing, next to his body heat.

"No more photos," he whispered. *Damnit! The battery will recover a little when it warms up, but will there be enough charge to show the pictures back at the cabin?*

"Let's go," said Wylie. He stowed the binoculars, tightened his rucksack, and downclimbed the slot they'd come up. Archimedes wasn't certain but he thought he'd seen a grin as he'd disappeared over the lip. His hands burned from rewarming, but the dexterity had returned and after a moment he followed Wylie down the slot.

Moving downhill and retracing their tracks, they made fast progress. About halfway back to the cabin Wylie called for a short break. Speaking softly, he began reciting what he'd seen of the complex and the cliff. He paused at times to ask Archimedes' perspective.

Archimedes listened to the details Wylie recalled. *Not only is he a remarkably agile climber but he has a sharp mind and knows his enemy well.*

"How long have you been in the war?"

"Two years. Signed up when I was eighteen," answered Wylie.

"You're twenty?"

"Yes."

Archimedes said nothing.

"I am," insisted Wylie.

"Okay," said Archimedes and smiled. *I don't believe him for a second.*

"Let's move," said Wylie and strode off in the snow.

They arrived at the cabin at around 9 PM. As soon as they were inside, Wylie announced that the cliff was a 'piece of cake'.

"Sure, it's almost vertical but it's got plenty of small trees," he said. The Scotsman and several Norwegians circled closer to listen.

Archimedes pulled out the phone and was relieved to note the battery icon: 15%. *I hope it's enough.* "We'll need to be quick, it's almost out of power," he said and put the phone down on the main table. The Scotsman and Torvald huddled over it. One of the Norwegians, named Varg, found a pencil and paper, and sat down at the table. Archimedes flipped through the photos on the screen to find the clearest ones and Varg began sketching as Wylie narrated the details of what they were seeing. Varg's left hand glided over the paper with a methodical, almost mechanical, grace, as he sketched and labelled several drawings.

The Scotsman was reviewing the drawings when he swore softly, looked at Torvald, and then called Stig over. "The bloody Gerries have now stationed an MG-42 and spotlights at the plant side of the suspension bridge."

Archimedes thought about the bridge he'd just seen — and Wylie's reaction to the machine gun — and couldn't stop himself from muttering that it would be like shooting fish in a barrel. No one liked the expression; especially the Norwegians. He wasn't sure if it was a linguistic or cultural issue. *Perhaps piscine metaphors are their territory.* Archimedes filed it under *Norwegian culture*, and vowed to tread lightly.

The Scotsman scowled, and then pursed his lips. After a few moments he said, "Good recon, lads. Go get some *scoff*." He pointed towards the room that had been co-opted as a mess hall. Archimedes picked up his phone and his stomach growled at the thought of warm stew as he followed Wylie towards the chow.

"Mate, that thing's the bee's knees! Never seen nothing like it," said Wylie. "Could really turn the tide of the war. Save a lot of lives, I reckon."

"Yes," said Archimedes, trying to think of a way to change the subject. *Wylie is sharp, young, a strong climber, and a kind-hearted soul — and, although he deserves it, I can't tell him that I'm from the future: it's too much.*

He cleared his throat. "Unfortunately, it's an experimental device and it's almost out of power. There are no more like it. It'll soon be useless."

"Yeah, well, the commander is keen on it — and you. He's raided the bugger Rommel in North Africa. And he always says, look for any way to succeed. I'd follow him anywhere," said Wylie. "Glad you're with us, mate. The Nazis don't know half the blow we're about to strike! It'll make the folks back home proud — although it's too late for some."

They ate for a while in silence. Periodically, Wylie glanced up to look at the commander, who was poring over the sketches in the main room.

"I reckon it'll be you and me leading the climb, mate," said Wylie.

"What?"

"I think the commander will select the cliff," said Wylie. "You and me are climbing partners." He held out his hand.

Tentatively, Archimedes reached out, shook Wylie's hand, and said, "You don't want to be my climbing partner: the last one died."

Wylie looked down into his bowl for a moment and then said, "Sorry to hear that. Recent, was it?"

"A… year ago," said Archimedes. "I only climb solo now."

"What happened?"

"He was leading a pitch on steep ice, and I was belaying. He had just finished putting in an ice screw, and was clipping in when he lost balance. I held the rope but he popped the screw, and the next two, like a zipper. He… fell about sixty feet and… when I got to him, he wasn't breathing… and there was blood… from his head." Archimedes' voice trembled. *This hurts so much.*

Breathe. Slow down and breathe. "I did everything I could, but—"

Wylie reached across the table and squeezed Archimedes' shoulder.

"Don't sound like you did anything wrong. Bad luck, is all," he said. "We need ya. I need ya,"

"I don't want the responsibility of lives depending on me."

"I didn't want to lose my brother to the Nazis during the Blitz, but I did."

"I'm not supposed to be here."

"None of us are," said Wylie. "But we have to defeat these monsters — otherwise nothing matters."

"You don't understand. I'm lost… this isn't my time." Archimedes throat tightened. *Am I trapped?*

"Listen, mate — like it or not, we've all got to do our part, but we never know what that is — or when it will be. The commander lost his own son three months ago on a raid *he* was leading, but you'd never know it by the way he acts," said Wylie. "You have to choose to keep moving forward, fighting the just fight. If you sit down in the snow and stop, you die."

Archimedes nodded. He knew the truth of Wylie's words — and wondered how such wisdom could come from a teenager. *The conditions in the crucible that forged him must have been harsh.*

He bedded down in his spot on the floor, and slept fitfully. In his dreams he saw his partner fall, and as he rushed over, the glacier suddenly shattered, and Archimedes fell into a gaping abyss —

He awoke with a racing heart, and breathed slowly to calm his mind from the lingering terror of his dreams. The cabin was quiet. He lay still and thought about the uncertainties tickling his brain — and after a moment he found the core: *Consequences*.

If I help Wylie lead the assault team up the cliff, I'm taking responsibility for men's lives — but because I'm in the past, are there further consequences? Will my actions change the future, my future, or is the past immutable and nothing I do matters?

Perhaps there is not one linear timeline but multiple instances of time and this is but one of many threads — and what happens here, now, dictates the future of this thread. But am I stuck in this version or could I jump to another thread? Heisenberg, Einstein, and Hawking might have a lively discussion — or maybe they are, somewhere — but how can I figure this out?

As his mind wrestled with the dilemma, his slow, rhythmic breathing washed away the adrenaline. His thoughts settled on the pragmatic. *I guess it comes down to this: do what's right in the moment because I can't possibly know the downstream implications. Assume my actions matter and do the right thing.*

Wylie is right; I have to help them.

He lay there a few more moments. Soon, men begin moving about the cabin and he arose to find another frigid, overcast sky. Archimedes shuffled into the kitchen area and helped himself to a bowl of oatmeal. He listened to the conversations around him and learned that Wylie was right: the cliff was to be the route of assault. This didn't really surprise him given the other options, but still caused him unease because he'd seen their sketchy climbing gear: hemp ropes, heavy alpenstocks, iron crampons, bulky flashlights, overstuffed canvas rucksacks, and hobnailed boots. *Sure, they're strong from hauling all this stuff around, but can they go up a steep cliff face with all the heavy gear and explosives? Wylie seemed to be the only climber in the group. Could the rest keep up? What happens if a man packing explosives falls?*

The ropes bothered Archimedes the most. He knew about the old-school hemp ropes: they were static, with no stretch or give; if you fell the rope would stop the fall, but you would be snapped in half. It was the equivalent of bungee jumping with a steel cable; it would pop your feet off your ankles, or just rip both legs off at the hips. Modern climbing ropes, like the one he carried, were dynamic and would stretch as they stopped a fall. But none of the team wanted anything to do with his fluorescent purple, nylon kernmantle rope. He tried explaining the advantages, and enthusiastically described the evolution of rope construction, but they all looked at him distrustfully.

It was particularly frustrating because he knew he was right. However, the realization that this was their time period, and not his, won out over the setback of being marginalized.

After noon, the commander called them all into the cabin to brief them on the timetable and details. He reviewed the timing and logistics of the assault plan and fielded questions.

"It's clear from the scouting report on the defensive positions that the Gerries think it daft that anyone would try to climb the cliff, so that's where we'll hit 'em from. It's critical that we get inside the electrolysis room without firing a shot or being discovered. Stealth is the only way, lads."

"How about getting *out*?" asked Point-man.

"Well, it's too tricky to escape back down the cliff after the charges go off. We won't have the time, so we'll go out along the rail line or scamper up to the plateau. It'll be after midnight so with speed on our part, and confusion on the Gerries' part — and a wee bit of luck — we can make a clean egress."

"If you can get aerial photos, why can't you just bomb the dam complex?" asked Archimedes. It seemed like a lot of unnecessary risk to sneak a commando team into an occupied country when you have the technology to just rain down death from above.

Stig stood, scowled at him, and said, "You are new so I can forgive your question. The weather is bad and the bombs fall wherever. You'll kill too many of our people!"

Immediately, Archimedes understood. This was long before GPS and smart bombs. A sufficient number of bombs would have to be dropped to ensure the destruction of the target but, given the error rate of the time period, the adjacent town would be pummeled or wiped out as well.

He looked around the cabin: a few wolves were showing their teeth, but there were no knives this time.

"Sorry," he said, and studied his feet.

The Scotsman wrapped up the meeting by saying, "Right, lads. We leave at sunset. Double check your kit and get some rest. We've a long night ahead."

Archimedes made an effort to rest, but soon gave up and paced around the cabin, watching the men check and pack gear, trying to keep out of the way and not ask questions. He overheard Wylie telling the commander that the assault team would not need the heavy mountaineering gear, such as crampons and alpenstocks, for the cliff. The loads they would carry were heavy enough and the extra equipment would not help the climb. *That's a relief.*

He moved on, and stopped to observe two men molding multiple lumps of something that looked like clay.

"Nobel 808," said one of the men, grinning. "Plastic explosive. Good stuff." He tossed a grapefruit-sized lump towards Archimedes — who jumped back, bobbling the catch, but snagged it before it hit the floor.

Peals of laughter broke out from both men and then spread around the cabin. One of the men held up a small tube, and said, "Harmless without the detonator." Then he elbowed the other man, who was still sniggering.

Archimedes felt warmth flood his face as he carefully handed the explosive back to the demolition man. He counted nine of the 'grapefruits', and something nagged at the back of his mind.

The charge I handled was less than a pound. They can't blow up a dam or even a small concrete building with these.

He continued his circuit around the cabin, and saw men counting out 45-caliber ammunition and loading magazines for the Thompsons and Colt pistols. He shivered when he saw a set of hemp ropes. And then it hit him. Earlier the commander had said *electrolysis room.*

The puzzle clicked into place. *They're going to destroy the heavy-water production facility. Holy shit! I've read about this raid — they're trying to stop the Nazis from developing the atomic bomb.*

❖

In the cold, dark hours of early evening, they left the cabin and followed a trail through the woods. The moon was brighter and the clouds thinner than the past few nights. Archimedes shuddered at the thought of what they would soon be attempting.

Several hours later, they arrived at the top of a steep hillside which led down to the gorge, separating them from the complex of buildings on top of the cliff. Here, they stopped to say their goodbyes. Six men would continue on the trail and circle up towards the plateau above the complex, and lay the groundwork for the planned escape overland to Sweden. Seven men, including Archimedes, would scale the cliff and assault the complex.

He watched their faces as they shook hands and exchanged good luck wishes. Quiet words of humor and encouragement were shared but Archimedes felt the tension and heaviness in the brief, cold, and somber parting. No one knew if the mission would be successful — or if any of them would see each other again.

Wylie stood next to Archimedes to watch the six men disappear into the woods. The Scotsman approached Archimedes and held out both hands. "Here," he said, handing him a Colt-45 pistol and a brass cylinder. "I'll not have you defenseless."

Archimedes accepted the weapon, and ejected the magazine to see that it was fully loaded. He slid it back into place, and verified the safety was on before securing the pistol in a zippered pocket. He then took the brass cylinder and examined it: a shell casing, with a screw top, and the word *Poison* — accompanied by a skull-and-crossbones — painted on the smooth cylinder.

"What's this?"

"Cyanide," answered the Scotsman. "You don't want to be captured alive by those bastards. Ever!"

"I'll remember that."

The Scot turned to beckon to the other men: Stig, Thorvald, Varg, Point-man, and one of the plastic-explosive jokers from earlier, a man named Llewelyn. Quietly, he said, "Twenty-one-hundred hours. Let's move, lads."

Archimedes was last in the line, as they proceeded down the steep hill navigating the hard packed and ice-crusted snow amongst the trees. At one point Llewelyn fell and Archimedes's heart leapt into his throat as he watched a dangerous slide unfold. Llewelyn managed to avert disaster by colliding with and grabbing a tree trunk. He looked shaken but was soon back on his feet. Archimedes exhaled slowly.

Within an hour they were at the partially ice-covered deep brook, then soon made their way across to the base of the cliff, where they paused to recheck and organize gear. The damp, frigid air bit deeply and Archimedes hugged himself against the cold. He trembled. *This is it.*

"Here you go," said the Scotsman and handed Archimedes a full canteen and six magazines for the Thompsons. "Everyone carries equal weight."

Archimedes nodded and stuffed these into his pack, though he was certain the commander's rucksack was the heaviest by far. The assault team huddled together against the rock and there was a faint jingling of metal buckles as they tightened the straps on their rucksacks.

"Go on, then. Up you go," said the Scot, putting his large hands on Wylie's and Archimedes' shoulders.

Archimedes took a deep breath and looked up the limestone crag. Ice covered some of the exposed rock, and snow pooled in folds and pockets. Scrub brush and stunted evergreens dotted the face higher up. He looked over at Wylie, who was pacing around and craning his neck to look upwards.

Wylie saw him and waved him over. "Here, what do you think of this line?" He pointed out landmarks as he named them and traced the route.

"Yeah, looks good," said Archimedes. "Lead on, brother."

Wylie moved fluidly upwards despite the 50-plus pounds on his back. *He looks like Spider-Man.* He followed Wylie up and discovered that there were many opportunities for solid handholds and foot placements — which would greatly help the team. *This is beautiful rock.*

Twenty feet up, he turned to look down and saw upturned faces watching him. One man was already scrambling up.

Archimedes' guts twisted at the thought of someone falling. He climbed higher, then looked down again to watch. His pulse pounded in his ears and he gripped the rock firmly – painfully. Responsibility gnawed at his emotions. Above him, Wylie disappeared over a lip.

Archimedes slowed his breathing. *I can do this; we can do this.* He resumed climbing and joined Wylie on a ledge, a hundred feet above the ground. "Bloody great, this is," said Wylie. "How are the others doing?"

"They're climbing like pros. Good route choice — it's like a ladder."

Wylie's boyish, gap-toothed smile flashed in the moonlight, then he disappeared upwards. The back of Archimedes' neck and arms began to tingle. And, although the frigid cold bit at his face and finger tips, his body felt warm and energized from the climbing. *This is amazing: I can't believe I'm here doing this.*

He looked out, down, and up — then grinned and climbed after Wylie. In a short period of time, they were into the section he'd seen from below, scattered with stunted trees and bushes. It was less steep here and the trunks and exposed roots provided firm holds and steps — provided they were tested before applying full body weight.

As they climbed higher, icy winds had steadily picked up, and now gusts blasted them. Because they were free climbing the cliff, they had no attachment to each other nor anchor points to the cliff: there was no rope or belayed protection to guard against a fall. *Fortunately this section is not as steep or exposed — this wind is rough.* Archimedes leaned out, holding onto two roots, and watched the climbing below.

A few men were clearly new to rock climbing and looked a little sketchy in their movements. One in particular appeared stiff and uncertain. *Relax, let it flow. You can do this.*

Despite the varied climbing experience, though, every member of the assault team shared the same critical personality elements for success. It wasn't a matter of bravado, swagger, or recklessness. It was *confidence*; an unshakeable belief that no matter how hard it got, they would make it work.

They also radiated camaraderie, a sense that together, they were so much stronger.

From Archimedes' perspective, the transition from a group of individuals that had their disagreements to an elite force was remarkable. He had never seen anything quite like it. It was as if moving up a dark, icy, nearly vertical 500-foot cliff was just a small thing that needed to be done, before sneaking into a guarded heavy-water production facility full of Nazis with guns, blowing the fucker up, and then getting the hell out. They would go up this cliff upside-down, if that's what it took.

He scrambled higher; just over halfway up now.

A strong gust of wind buffeted Archimedes, and he stopped moving to keep solid contact. Wylie was waiting for him just above, holding securely on to a trunk of an evergreen tree about the diameter of his arm. When

Archimedes arrived he said, "Your turn to lead. But let's wait for the lads to catch up."

Archimedes surveyed the immediate route above and decided to move to the right to bypass a double-decker-bus-sized quartzite nose sticking out. He sidestepped underneath it and found a chimney, with what looked like good holds. He looked below at the men climbing up. Free climbing had the advantage of speed, but at greater risk — and since they were all closely following the same line, anyone falling would take out a man or two, or a whole group.

He paused to slow his breathing and rest his muscles.

Archimedes thought of actions and consequences. The US would ultimately unleash uranium and plutonium bombs on Hiroshima and Nagasaki. He didn't know what would happen if the raid were to fail but knew he must do everything possible to stop the Nazis from getting such a terrible weapon. *I wish no one had ever figured out how to wreak that level of devastation. But I can only change what's in front of me.*

The wind blasted him out of his musings and he chastised himself. *Concentrate! If I fall or do something dumb to alert the guards, then the whole mission will fail: Nazi Germany might win the race for the bomb.*

Archimedes' new timeline, if such a thing were possible, might be one in which London was the first city to become a nuclear slag-heap, followed by Paris or New York. His teammates did not know how far advanced the German scientists had come in the development of intercontinental ballistic missiles. The Allies would soon experience the devastation of the V-2, but none would truly appreciate the gap in Axis missile technology until after the war. He shuddered from more than the cold, and snapped back to focus on the next segment.

My lead. Make it count.

He stemmed up the chimney. The weight of the pack dug the straps painfully into his shoulders. A minute later, forearm muscles burning, he crested above the quartzite nose and looked up. Only a hundred or so more feet to go. He surveyed to find the best way up the next segment, and balked at the first two candidates: on one, the rock looked too smooth; on the other there were too few shrubs and small trees to provide good handholds. The third line looked like good rock, but it was significantly steeper than what they'd climbed so far. He and Wylie could do this last segment without much difficulty, but what of the men below?

He chose the steeper segment and made steady progress upwards. Lungs burned from the cold and muscles complained from the exertion. When he arrived at the top of the cliff he crept over the edge, breathing heavily. Exhilaration tingled along his spine. *I feel so alive!*

He looked down to watch Wylie's progress, then turned towards the complex of buildings beyond a fence topped with razor wire. He did not see any guards. Closer to the fence was a depression in the rock several feet deep, with good concealment. He crawled over to it and tried to make himself as small as possible as he surveyed the perimeter fence and the facilities beyond.

Wylie was soon at his side, and looked at the concrete buildings through his binoculars. He studied for several minutes and then crawled back over to the edge of the cliff and looked down. Archimedes saw him tense up and look from side to side, and felt a sinking sensation. He belly-slid over to Wylie to find out what was wrong.

"Llewelyn's in a spot of bother," said Wylie. "He's not moving. Last segment might be too steep for him."

"Rope?"

"Aye."

Archimedes retrieved the rope that he'd been told not to use from his backpack. He secured one end around a thigh-sized tree stump at the edge of the cliff, and tied it off. He then parsed out the rope, tying a figure-of-eight knot on a bight every four feet. A nine-millimeter rope was simply too thin to try to pull oneself up by hand or grasp with legs. Although it seemed a little counter-intuitive that one couldn't directly climb a climbing rope, they were designed for anchoring, attaching to harnesses, and rappelling. The technique for climbing vertically involved Prusik cords, loops that provided a sliding friction knot on the rope to climb straight up. But they didn't have time to teach this technique nor the gear to do so, so Archimedes made loop-knots large enough for Llewelyn, and the others to use as hand and toe holds, to get up this last bit safely.

When he had finished, he tossed the rope over the edge and Wylie downclimbed. One hundred feet below, he could see Wylie communicating with Llewelyn. Before long, Llewelyn started up the steep section, walking himself up the rock, pulling hand over hand on the knots. He soon crested the rim, white-eyed, unslung his Thompson and rucksack, crawled quickly away from the edge, and sprawled out, prostrate and panting. He looked back over his shoulder and made eye contact with Archimedes. "Thanks, mate. I bloody hate heights," he said.

Soon, the Scotsman and the Norwegians were at the top, and Wylie scampered up last. Hidden in the depression, they crouched and redistributed the gear they'd hauled up; Archimedes added his load to the pile. Then, in hushed voices, they reviewed the plan. Varg would open the gate with bolt cutters. Torvald and Stig would gain access to the locked concrete building housing the heavy-water electrolysis cells. After the charges had been set, they would signal the egress. Everyone was instructed to follow their assignments, and to be alert.

Archimedes watched them all slink off into the night. Soon Varg was at the gate and cut the chain quickly and quietly with a huge pair of bolt cutters. Stig and Torvald snuck through the open gate.

A loud boom sounded from the top of the electrolysis building, and from his hidden lookout position he saw everyone freeze.

A guard emerged from the adjacent main building and looked around. Torvald and Stig ducked behind a collection of pressurized tanks, pipes, and valves. The guard strolled around, peering, and then another boom echoed from above. It was the hydrogen burners setting and then restarting; a normal occurrence at the plant. Torvald had explained that the guards stopped reacting to the explosive backfire after a few weeks of being at the plant, so this guard must be a newcomer. After a moment he went back inside.

Torvald and Stig stole across the plant yard and then scaled up to the roof of the electrolysis building. Archimedes knew the next phase would be tricky. The two Norwegians were going to crawl down to the locked hydrolysis room through a long conduit that extended to the roof of the building. Once inside, they would plant linked plastic-explosive charges onto the heavy-water electrolysis production units and storage tanks. Exiting, whether by door or window, would have to be quick, as they were using a two-minute fuse. *Not enough time.* After lighting the fuse, they would have to run like hell. Archimedes imagined them flying out of the building door or through a window like in clichéd scenes in movies: *Hey guys, we've got to get out of here right now! This thing's gonna blow!*

The rest of the plan, the egress of the teams, depended upon where they were when the explosions started, and upon the German military response. Archimedes had been told to stay where he was, with the rope in place, just in case it was needed. If no one came back this way he was to untie it and climb back down the cliff as fast as possible, and get away. Varg, the artist and bolt-cutter, would leave a Thompson submachine gun on the ground by the gate to make sure the Nazis knew it was a British commando raid. This would hopefully prevent the executions of Norwegian citizens in retaliation.

After the sabotage, some of the team would cross-country ski 250 miles to cross the border into neutral Sweden. Others would lay low in adjacent villages. Archimedes was on his own. Besides getting down the cliff, he would have to make it to the address Torvald made him memorize. Both Torvald and the commander had warned him that the Gestapo would torture him to no end. Thus, the pistol and cyanide.

Archimedes crouched in his frozen stance. He wasn't sure if they were over schedule, but there hadn't been any gun shots, klaxons, or spotlights.

The door to the building banged open and the two Norwegians came running out with buoyant strides, and pumped fists in the air, signaling to the other teams that it was time to go.

Forty-five seconds later, there was a boom and then rolling echoes that sounded like thunder, and vibrations shook the limestone under Archimedes' hands and feet.

And —

The Germans did nothing. There was no response.

The explosion didn't sound all that different to Archimedes than the hydrogen burners that had blasted earlier, but he felt the difference in the sonic wave, deep in the rock. He watched the Allied teams flow away into the night. Some followed a trail to the top of the mountain. Others crossed the narrow suspension bridge, which he thought was pretty ballsy until he noticed there weren't any guards manning the machine gun or the spotlight. Archimedes also noticed that none of the Allied teams were coming back in his direction.

He untied and coiled the rope and then assembled his pack for descent. He looked below at the downclimb, and then across the yard to the main building. Still quiet. Thirty minutes had passed.

Then a guard burst out from the main building, running. He tripped and fell but soon he was followed by a dozen more, all sprinting in different directions. They were all yelling. It was the military barracks version of an anthill that had been poked with a stick. Archimedes decided it was probably time to — what was the British expression? — bugger off. *Yes, definitely time to bugger off.*

He began downclimbing. Over halfway down, he heard angry shouts from directly above, and then a light shone on him.

"Halt," came a command, which he ignored and quickened his descent. The light followed him and there came the angry buzzing of a German machine pistol. Some of the bullets kicked off the limestone a meter to the right of his head. A shard grazed Archimedes' forehead, and blood trickled into his right eye.

More lights appeared, and Archimedes was pinned by the intersections of the beams. He kept perfectly still and looked down. His panted exhalations plumed in the bright light. One hundred feet below, the partially ice-covered brook roared.

"Halt!"

"Nicht schiessen!" yelled Archimedes, and slowly raised one arm.

He paused to calculate, counted to three, and then kicked backwards off the cliff, rotating in the air.

They fired.

Archimedes executed a slow backflip and sped downwards, feet first.

He hit the ice and plunged through.

Archimedes awoke shivering in his tent. He was lying on top of his sleeping bag, soaking wet, disoriented, and in pain; his right ankle screamed. He lay motionless on his back, panting, and blinked at the fluorescent orange glow of the tent fabric. He realized that it must be daylight outside. *What happened?*

He sat up slowly, wincing in pain, and looked around the tent: there his sleeping bag; his socks hanging from a line; his isobutane stove; and his clothes in the corner. His head throbbed. He reached up and felt the wound on his forehead and the matted hair stuck to it.

Archimedes extended his arm, unzipped the entrance, and looked out. The tent was perched on a rocky outcrop overlooking a blinding white glacier – the same spot he remembered selecting as a campsite. *But how many days ago was that? What's happened to me?*

I remember falling, and then Norway and the raid on the Nazi heavy-water facility, and then falling...

But maybe I just dreamed the whole thing. I must've fallen while climbing and hit my head, and then somehow made it back to camp in a concussed stupor.

He knew that this was the only realistic explanation for what had happened, but it felt *wrong*. His emotions pushed back against the cold logic. He began shivering again and let the tent flap fall, and turned to look for some dry clothes and his parka. When he pulled over his pack, he felt something heavy and bulky in one of the zippered pockets: inspecting it, he found a semi-automatic Colt 45 pistol, and the brass cyanide container.

What the hell! It was real. All of it!

He heard distant voices and pulled the flap aside. The glare off the glacier blinded him and he couldn't see the source of the noise, until he retrieved his sunglasses and located three people, less than a quarter of a mile away, walking towards him.

Soon they disappeared out of view, hidden by shadows of the ridge upon which he was camped. The next time Archimedes saw them, they were standing in front of him.

"Are you Archimedes Jackson?" asked a squat guy with a huge pack.

"Yes."

"We're part of a search and rescue team. You were reported overdue two days ago. We set out yesterday to look for you and then your emergency beacon came on this morning. Everything okay?"

"Had a fall and hit my head. I think I broke my ankle," said Archimedes.

"You look pretty beat up," said a lanky man, and unslung a pack with a red-cross logo. "Let's take a look at you." He knelt beside Archimedes and opened his pack. The third guy took out a handheld radio and began chatting with someone.

Archimedes blinked up at the blue sky, and heard boots crunch towards him.

"Chopper's on the way," said a voice.

The doctors put screws and plates in his ankle to repair the fractures. Archimedes spent several days in the hospital, begging to be let out. It wasn't that they were deliberately mistreating him, he simply wanted independence and solitude. Besides, hospitals were basically not where any rational human would want to spend any time. *Good thing I didn't pick medicine as a career.*

An old climbing buddy, Fred, came to rescue him from the hospital. Archimedes had to endure the wheelchair-ride-of-shame to the curb, before being allowed to crutch over to the truck, three feet away, under the sympathetic — but unwanted — gazes of Fred and a hovering medical assistant. He grunted as he slid into the passenger seat.

The July sky was a spectacular, deep arctic blue with wispy puffs of cumulous clouds. The overabundance of daylight and the mild summer weather energized the denizens of Anchorage, who had to endure so much darkness and cold throughout the winter. It was as if the population were bipolar, chained to the cycles of daylight and darkness. Right now, everyone was manically chatty and buzzing with verve. Even before his climbing trip it had been getting on his nerves – now it felt doubly so.

As they drove towards Archimedes' cabin, Fred told a few jokes and then began *the inquisition* with a few polite observations. Archimedes just stared out of the passenger window. Fred soon bridged into softball inquiries, which Archimedes knew were a warm-up to the more detailed ones to come. Largely, he didn't feel like answering anything: the hospital had exhausted his tolerance for questions. He muttered a few replies, then pretended to fall asleep. They cruised the interstate out of Anchorage in silence.

The truck bounced up the long gravel drive to the cabin, jostling Archimedes' leg painfully. When the jarring stopped, Fred helped Archimedes inside to sit on the couch in the family room. Fred got a fire going. Then, after hanging a full kettle, he turned and said, "So what happened? And why the hell were you climbing that route alone — especially after last year with Kel dying on Mount—"

"Not now, Fred!" Archimedes said, cutting him off, and then drew in a deep breath. "Please. I appreciate everything you do for me and you're a good friend, but I'm feeling sick. If you want to pour yourself some coffee when that's done boiling, that'd be great. I know you have stuff to do. Me, I'm going to gimp my ass to bed. Thanks for driving me home."

"Sure," said Fred, and rose stiffly. He walked to the door and put his hand on the knob. "Look, Arky, you have to let go to live. You have to move forward. Just know I'm always here for you, man."

The door closed behind him.

Archimedes rose and used a single crutch to hobble to his office: oak bookshelves from floor to twelve-foot ceiling bracketed three sides of the large space. In front of the large picture-frame window occupying the fourth wall was the large, polished cedar desk that Archimedes had built. Above it hung three large flat-panel computer displays. Heavy, rolled survey maps were neatly stacked in a wooden column at the edge of the desk.

He sat at the desk and for many minutes did not move. A wave of conflicting emotions battled within him — finally settling on regret.

Archimedes extracted his phone and dialed.

"Hello," answered Fred. "Everything okay?"

"No," said Archimedes. "Fred, I'm sorry. I've treated you and everyone else like dirt. I've dwelled in self-pity too long and ignored the people who matter to me. Everything you've been telling me is true... I just didn't want to hear it."

"Arky, you've pushed everyone who cares about you away."

"I see that now," said Archimedes. "Is the offer to go fishing still good? I haven't seen your new boat."

"Of course, man. Boat's not so new — the invite was months ago."

"I'm sorry."

"How about this weekend — before summer's completely gone?" asked Fred. "If the orthopedist will let you, of course. We can prop you up in the back. There's a great comfy seat with cushions."

"Yes. I'd like that very much."

"Awesome. I'll call you tomorrow. Give a holler if you need anything from town."

"Thanks, Fred."

After hanging up, he limped over to a section in the bookshelf, and pulled up a stool. He eased himself down, and scanned through his curated section of mountaineering books, mostly old and out of print. *I know it's here. And I know I've seen him.*

Gotcha!

Archimedes pulled out a thick tome and opened it; he began flipping through the glossy pages, which were a mixture of text and black-and-white photos. The book was a compendium of the triumph on Everest in 1953. He ignored the spectacular photos on the summit, shot by Sir Edmund Hillary and Tenzing Norgay, and flipped past all the photos of Hillary and Norgay.

Finally, he came across a picture of a bunch of sunburnt mountaineers and sherpas, arm-in-arm, smiling like Cheshire cats. He looked closely at each face. Along the back row, fifth from the left, was a climber with a gap-toothed grin. The saliva dried in Archimedes' mouth, his heart pounded, and his spirit leapt. *It's him!*

He moved his index finger along the text as he read the caption of the support climbers and sherpas: the men who hauled the gear, set the routes, and built the high camps. He couldn't believe it. That was really him in the picture; Lieutenant Wylie Dankworth.

Only two people made that first summit, of course — and gained the stardom — but everyone knew, then and now, that it required a lot of support and a well-run team. And there was Wylie grinning, as proudly as Archimedes remembered him in 1943.

Holy shit, I knew he would be there.

His joy suddenly vanished. *Is there still time?*

He stumbled over to his desk and booted up the computer. He pulled his desk chair over and sat — and waited. The computer finally welcomed him with a login screen and he pulled the keyboard over and tapped through the security. He opened a search window and typed: *Wylie Dankworth Everest 1953.*

He scrutinized the results, and began fiercely clicking and typing. Several hours passed. Archimedes missed his scheduled pain pills. He kept digging. The phone rang. He ignored it. His stomach grumbled for food and he felt lightheaded.

He stopped to refuel. Then, after coffee and a peanut-butter-and-jelly sandwich, he was right back at the computer.

There.

He thumbed on his smartphone and dialed. There were a series of clicks and then a ringtone.

"Hello."

"Wylie?"

"Speaking."

"It's Archimedes."

Pause.

Finally, a gravelly voice said, "Good Lord. It's been... donkey's years. I didn't know if you'd survived the war... I tried to find you but no one knew anything. Where've you been? How are you?"

"I've been lost, but I found my way," said Archimedes.

"Bloody hell, you were lost when we found ya," cackled Wylie.

"Yes, I was," said Archimedes, and laughed, too. He wondered where to begin. "I want to hear about what happened after the raid. How did the lads do? Then I want to hear all about the '53 Everest expedition. And all about you."

Wylie coughed and wheezed, then said, "You sound exactly like I... remember... but you must be, oh... a hundred years old or more." Coughing interrupted him again. "I'm 92… I lied when I told you I was 20." He giggled and then had another coughing fit.

"I guess time has been kind to me," said Archimedes. "And I think I understand now. Things you helped me see. I feel blessed to have had you as a climbing partner. I'm sorry we didn't get to climb together after the war."

"Aye. Me too, mate… me too."

As they chatted about the raid and the years that had followed, tears flowed down Archimedes' cheeks.

KLICKITAT

Esmond discovered the circle of skeletal remains less than a mile from the intended camp, and motioned for a halt. He and his partner dropped their fifty-pound mountaineering packs. The bleached bones would have been lost in the white noise of the Mazama Glacier were it not for the contrast of the black, flat-topped basalt rock onto which they were precisely arranged.

Esmond approached it, boot-falls creaking in the frigid snow.

It was some sort of triad. Three thick femurs, angled with three smaller, long bones, each ending in a hoof or foot. In the center was a skull. And a ring of horns.

Flipping weird. What the fuck is this?

He looked over at his wife. *Maybe she shouldn't see this. We wanted to get away from death.*

Her amber reflective sunglass lenses looked back at him. Gianna slid her white balaclava down. Above her smooth, coppery skin and aquiline nose, several hair wisps escaped her wool cap and fluttered in the breeze.

She is so beautiful.

Esmond got out his camera to take a few pictures of his wife.

He motioned to her and studied her face for any reaction as she approached. She looked as tired as he felt. After several steps, she stopped and propped her sunglasses up. Her green eyes locked on his with alert curiosity.

She resumed walking and stopped next to him. He turned to the bones. "What do you make of this, love?"

"Dunno. Kids? Dumbasses?" Gianna suggested.

"Hmm. Not sure."

He took three photos of the skeletal arrangement and then put the camera away. *This is not the realm for kids or dumbasses.*

Mount Adams is a frequently climbed stratovolcano; the second highest peak in Washington State. Not far from Seattle, Washington and Portland, Oregon; it could draw some crowds, but not this route. Few came to this side of the mountain; especially since the forest fire, a decade ago. Road access to the nearest trailhead had been wiped out, changing the approach to Sunrise Camp into a long, grueling, trail-less slog. Kids and dumbasses just didn't venture here. Besides the ass-dragging haul to camp, the summit routes were more difficult. This side was too far, too remote, and too difficult for the casual trekker or climber.

The South Spur route is where everyone goes. The long ski slope attracts 99 percent of climbing traffic; camping out at the Lunch Counter, where a clown-pants array of brightly-colored tents of various sizes competed for flat space on the rock-rimmed snow shelf. Of the glaciers, rock-cleavers, and routes on Adams, the South Spur offered the least risk. Not zero, just not bad.

In the summer you could camp with a hundred of your besties. Wake up. Strap on your crampons and join the big conga line to the summit. Strings of people plodding toward the pyramid top, like in Hollywood movies depicting the times of the Pharaohs. Get a clear, sunny forecast, especially on a holiday or weekend, and the population tripled. One could — on any given ultraviolet radiation scorching sojourn — participate with hundreds of your fellow humans: eyebrows singed; lips and nose-tips blistered; and teeth whitened. Don't forget the 10,000 SPF; apply every ten minutes during the climb to be sure. Make it to the summit, celebrate, and glissade or ski (if you brought them) your way back down.

It is not an easy climb. No, it's a big mountain and it's a long-haul to the summit (12,276 ft). But it just isn't a technical climb. Dogs run up and down it.

But they were on the mountain in the spring, months before the climbing season really started, and on a different glacier, with a large ridge sticking up like a rock mohawk, separating them from the other side. There wasn't anyone around; they were completely alone.

Except — someone put the circle of bones here.

Why does it look familiar? Esmond couldn't place it, but an image hovered in his mind. Shaking off the thought, he grunted that they should get going. He shouldered his pack by squatting like a sumo-wrestler, balancing the pack on his knee and gently easing one arm into a strap, then allowing the pack to slide gently into place. Trying to scoop, twist, and throw a heavy load onto your back was a recipe for a lumbar sprain or worse.

Standing, he plodded forward and up. Gianna followed wordlessly in his boot-tracks.

Esmond looked back once. *I've seen this before, but where?*

Sunrise Camp, 8,500 ft

Sunrise Camp was a mound of rocks and earth that rose just a little above the Mazama Glacier, off to the side. Gianna set her pack down next to Esmond's; in the dirt, near a circle of rocks. There were several of these campsites, all unoccupied, ready and waiting, constructed by previous climbers who'd stayed the night here. Relatively level spots had been selected and a ring of rocks had been built up at the edge as a wind break. Some sites only had a low wall, like irregular loaves of bread dropped on the ground; others stood three feet high, rocks carefully chocked in like puzzle pieces and added to by successive occupants. Some climbers were like masons and really got into the art of it all.

The wind, steadily rising, gusted, pushing volcanic dirt from the campsite and out onto the glacier. Gianna was glad to be free of the pack and stretched her sore back.

Esmond had selected a good site, sheltered as best as possible from the wind. He went to work setting up the parabolic mountaineering tent. Gianna watched his lean, tall frame extend the two Z-folding, segmented tent poles to their full lengths and begin to thread them into the fluorescent orange nylon. She imagined her husband's upper-back and arm muscles rippling under the layers of clothes as he worked.

Gianna retrieved the camping stove from her pack, screwed the burner onto the red isobutane canister, and set it down behind a windbreak, just outside the camp circle. She managed to dodge a flailing aluminum tent pole as Esmond wrestled with it from halfway inside the partially-erect, flapping nylon. There were a few rocks next to the spot she chose for the stove, ideal for sitting upon, making this a fine kitchen. Taking two five-liter bags, she walked over to the glacier to gather snow.

Returning, she filled the one-liter aluminum pot, lit the stove, and placed the container on the burner. Melting snow for drinking water and cooking wasn't exciting, but it was necessary. It invariably involved numb fingers — or burnt ones, if you weren't careful.

She thought about tomorrow

Alpine start in pitch dark. Up at 3 am. Headlamps. Pee. Quick coffee. Snack. Pack check. Pee again. And go.

Their intended route on the Klickitat Glacier, up past The Castle, eventually joined the South Spur route near the summit.

She sighed. *Few see this beautifully rugged side of the mountain.*

Her musings did not distract her from periodically adding more snow to the melting concoction. But her thoughts and gaze drifted higher, up the mountainside, to The Castle.

She stared at it: a tall, crenelated turret seemingly from medieval times. The raven-black specter disappeared as clouds and mist rolled by — but then reappeared. A natural cylindrical rock formation with a flat top an acre across, it rose from the crest of Battlement Ridge like an evil tower from a Tolkien novel; dark and brooding.

The Castle vanished again and Gianna went back to her preparations. Esmond finished inside the tent, emerged, and began tying off guy lines to metal stakes that he pounded into the earth with an ice-hammer, or by looping the line around larger rocks.

Gianna called out, "Hey, honey. What would you like for dinner? Freeze-dried Texas chili or freeze-dried Jamaican jerk chicken?" She held aloft two sealed, bulletproof, use-by-the-end-of-this-century meal pouches.

Esmond laughed. "How about homemade veggie lasagna, Pinot Noir, and fresh-baked cherry pie with coffee ice cream?"

"Sure. You can just trot your little bottom down to the car and drive a few hundred miles. I'll wait."

Lines finished and inspected, Esmond stood and walked over to the 'kitchen' and squatted down on a rock next to Gianna. "Naaaaaah," he said, emulating a goat.

The goat noise killed the conversation.

Gianna added another handful of snow to the stove pot, which was groaning and creaking from the expansion of heating metal, and hissing underneath from the flow of hot gas. Gianna thought about the bones they'd seen lower on the mountain.

"Seriously. What was that back there?" she asked.

"A *triskelion*. I think. I wasn't sure, but it came back to me, from a Classics course in college."

"Didn't you get a C-minus?"

"C-plus," he said, flinging a small rock which bounced and clattered on the field talus next to camp. He continued, "It's an ancient symbol. The Greeks borrowed a triple, swirly-lines icon from Neolithic times, thousands of years before them, and changed it. *Triskeles*; three-legged. This became the go-to brand for the tyrants of Syracuse."

"Rock band?"

"Someone is sleeping outside the tent tonight, methinks," he said. "No. The tyrants of Syracuse were murderous, Greek control freaks who ruled over the island of Sicily for several centuries — a couple of hundred years B.C."

Gianna withheld another barb and let him continue.

"The triskelion adopted by the tyrants had the head of a Gorgon at the center, with three running legs projecting out."

"A Gorgon?"

"Yep. Medusa was one of the three Gorgons you hear about. You know, poisonous snakes for hair. Gaze turns people to stone. Scary fangs. And in some stories, demon-wings and snake-scales."

"Cool. I bet they had awesome cereal boxes back then. Grab a bowl of super-sugar-coated Hop-Lites. Don't look at the Medusa, kids."

He chuckled.

"The bones back there were from three different animals. Goat, cougar, and elk," he said, and threw another clattering rock.

"Jesus," she exclaimed.

The wind rose. Mist billowed up, then tentacled and whipped through the saddle of the ridge. The high cirrus haze above darkened. An observer looking up from way below in the valley, in bright sunshine, would see lenticular clouds blossoming and shrouding the upper third of the great mountain. Concentric, elliptical, and streaming; like dancing pipe-smoke rings.

Gianna reached for her hard-shell jacket, and slid it on against the cold wind, cinching up the hood. Looking up, she saw the sun angling to set. It was just above the horizon, where Mount Hood in Oregon stood proud — shrouded in her own lenticulars — and just below the expanding dark cloud above.

The unmistakeable *clack* of rockfall from above made them both turn. Gianna couldn't see where it came from but Esmond pointed to Suksdorf Ridge. Gianna got out the Zeiss monocular to look. Light and dark bands played across the ridge from streaming clouds in the setting sun.

From her spot, the Mazama Glacier swooped up; an exponential curve, flat near camp, and then angling up, ever steeper towards the skyline. The slow-moving river of ice, hundreds of feet thick, showed crevasse cracks and dots of rockfall. Near the top, Gianna could see the bergschrund — a deep butcher-knife slice, separating the glacier from the mountain. The shadowy maw split almost the full width of the face, like a death rictus.

Another loud crack. Further away and to the right this time. Gianna swiveled the monocular to the location of the sound and adjusted the focal range, then saw a rock crash and launch into the air from its collision with the ridge below The Castle.

"Castle," she said.

She scanned up its walls and studied the curious rock formations surrounding the flat, round top. The crenellated spikes gave The Castle a Statue of Liberty look.

She handed the monocular to Esmond, removed the aluminum pot from the stove, and poured the hot water — the fourth liter — into the last of the containers. She sealed the screw-on lid, stooped, grabbed, and stood. She walked over to the tent, and then ducked inside, careful to keep her boots outside, and stuffed two each into the depths of the two sleeping bags.

Each bag sat atop a whisper-thin, inflatable pad with reflective silver material on one side. Both needed inflating. At 1.5 miles above sea level, blowing these up — with pursed lips, exhaling large lungfuls of air — invariably generated a combination of lightheadedness, numb mouth and hands, and hypoxia-induced retinal flashes. After regaining blood pH and O_2 equilibrium, she arranged some clothes and prepped her side of the tent.

Finished, she exited the tent. Another tumble of rocks crashed from high on the mountain.

Esmond was still studying The Castle. She walked over to him in their makeshift kitchen.

"Looks like Hecate, goddess of gateways, witchcraft, ghosts and probably a few other things I can't recall. She had a spiked crown like Lady Liberty, and was often depicted as a triple form," he said.

"Why is it you couldn't recall all this stuff for your Classics final twenty years ago, and now we can't shut you up? It's a little creepy."

He shrugged and threw another rock. "Dunno."

Gianna set about melting more snow. She fiddled with her necklace. Esmond had given it to her, and a bracelet, to match the engagement ring. All made of titanium — which was the only metal Gianna could wear without breaking out in a blistering, peeling rash. Later, for fun, Esmond had surprised her with a titanium ice axe. To complete the set, he had said, laughing. She smiled at the memory and watched him work. *He really is thoughtful and kind.*

She watched him, hunched over their packs, beginning to lay out technical gear for their climb: one hundred meters of nine-mm climbing rope; six ice screws; an assortment of screw-lock carabiners; two belay devices; several aluminum pickets; a pulley for crevasse rescue; Prusik cords; four ice axes (his and hers lengths; including Gianna's special one); and short lengths of cord and slings. To this array he added their harnesses and crampons. She watched him carefully consider each piece and then stop and stare up into space. She suspected he was lost in thought, visualizing the route; imagining different scenarios and what climbing hardware might be needed where.

A bubbling noise brought her attention back to the stove, and she poured two cups of boiling water into each of the freeze-dried meal pouches. Folding the tops over, she squeezed the bottoms a few times to mix the contents, and looked at the titanium GPS chronometer on her wrist.

"Ten minutes to din-dins," she announced.

"OK. I'm going to head east to get a better look at the upper Klickitat. See ya in ten," he said, and turned to walk downhill, weaving through boulders.

After dinner by the light of their LED headlamps, they prepped for bed. Gianna set her watch alarm and snuggled deep into her sleeping bag. The small tent was not quite long enough for Esmond's tall frame so he positioned himself at an angle as he slid into his bag.

He dimmed his headlamp and stuffed it into a mesh pouch at the inside top of the tent. The wind buffeted the tent and the lamp swung gently, casting shifting shadows on the walls. Esmond was lost in thought and lay still listening to the gusts.

After several minutes he said, "Hopefully the weather will hold tomorrow."

"Yes. How'd the route look?"

"Good."

After a long pause Gianna said, "I'm glad we're doing this climb."

Esmond rolled over to look at Gianna. "Me too, love. It's healthy for us, especially with all that we've been through."

"Thank you for supporting me."

"Of course, love. We're in this together," he said. "We'll get pregnant again." He leaned close and gave her a kiss on the cheek.

Gianna smiled and looked into his eyes. Esmond felt an aching in his chest. *I love her so much. Even through the pain she can smile.* "I love you."

"I love you too, Esi."

She placed her head on his chest. Esmond reached up and turned off the lamp. He pulled her close.

Winds rose and fell as he drifted off to sleep.

3 am

At the chirping of Gianna's watch, Esmond grunted from within his mummy bag. Wind buffeted the tent. Silently, he counted thirty heartbeats and then poked his wife with a gentle elbow through the bag. Volumes of information communicated with one simple nudge: silence the alarm, get up, get ready, let's go.

Esmond shimmied on pants, a Merino wool sweater, and a soft-shell jacket over the base layers. He unzipped the tent, slid his butt towards the opening to poke his socked feet outside, and wrestled on cold boots. He reached back and pulled on the red, goose-down puffy, rocked forward to sit on his haunches outside, and re-zipped the tent. The cold bit his face, and he slid up his balaclava and pulled up the hood of the puffy; securing it against the wind.

Above, the gibbous moon played hide-and-seek with bands of clouds scurrying across the heavens. Moonlight bathed the camp in a mosaic of sharp shadows alternating between a grainy green glow and grey darkness. Chinook winds blew across the glacier and whistled through the barren rocky landscape that framed the sides of the massive ice river.

Since it first erupted 500,000 years ago, weather and the slow but inexorable advance of the millions of tons of crushing ice in the twelve named glaciers had shaped and carved this mountain. Subsequent volcanic events had poured out more molten rock to add to the mass, and then the glaciers had got to work again. The most recent magma-bubbling spew had been over a thousand years ago. Most scientists considered this mountain to be dormant. But the mountain didn't care; it was indifferent to the thoughts and lives of humans.

A swirl of a million stars appeared in a gap above, until a large squid-ink black cloud crept across, blotting out all light and plunging the camp into darkness. Esmond extracted another headlamp, thumbed it on, and snugged the stretchy band around his wool cap. He trudged over to a boulder at the edge of the camp, and peed.

A low keening wail drifted through the camp. Esmond stopped still to listen to the rising and falling notes. *Must be currents of air playing in the holes and channels in the lava rock.*

A zipping sound brought his attention to Gianna as she emerged from the tent, yawning and complaining about the cold. Her headlight beam flicked towards him, and she walked over to the kitchen. She soon had the stove on, and a pot of snow on top. Her exhaled breath condensed into vapor before the wind snatched it away.

"Looks like we may strike out on the weather."

"Great," grunted Gianna, shoulders sagging.

"It was supposed to be clear, but we'll be fine unless it's howling up there," he said.

Esmond looked at his watch: 3:15 am. Gianna dumped freeze-dried coffee crystals into cups of hot water, and passed one over to Esmond. They both sipped as they prepped and rechecked gear. Hands numbed quickly in the cold, so gloves stayed on except for dexterity-intensive tasks. Munching a chocolate peanut-butter ball that Gianna had made for this trip, Esmond reiterated the plan and timetable.

At 3:35 he finished securing crampons to his boots and looked over at Gianna.

He was about to ask her if —

"Ready," she said.

"OK."

He hoisted his pack, and they set off on a short downhill. Headlights swept ahead and the metal claws strapped to their boots crunched over the lava rock. Just one rocky section to cross and they would soon be on the glacier.

Gianna called for a halt to adjust some gear. Esmond shifted his weight from foot to foot to keep blood flowing. His LED headlight highlighted his left boot as he looked down at his feet. The twelve metal spikes haloed around the boot cast odd shadows. *Like the crown of Hecate.*

They finished ascending the rock ramp at the snout of the glacier, and stepped onto the Klickitat Glacier. The pre-dawn glow was just enough to see the outline of the mountain and the dim sky. Clouds built, and the 10,000 ft cloud deck skimmed just above the black rock tower on the right.

Esmond grunted with the uphill effort.

Further along, they stopped to rope up. The angle had kicked up enough that they needed the security to guard against a fall. It wasn't just falling down the slope they had to worry about. They also had to worry about falling *into* the slope, if they stumbled over a crevasse. These could be obvious gaping slots, which were easy to avoid; or they might be hidden under a thin snow crust, like a trap door ready to spring and drop a climber 100 ft into the glacier. You would fall until you hit the bottom or until you wedged in a narrow spot where the ice walls converged. Climbers called it *corking*.

"The upper spots I could see looked pretty filled in yesterday, but there's always more slots than you know," said Esmond. He probed a slight depression in the snow for signs of a lurking crevasse, as Gianna belayed from a metal anchor she had pounded into the glacier a safe distance back.

Satisfied, he waved Gianna forward. While waiting, he felt the glacier grind and pop under his feet. The rooted metal spikes of the crampons conducted the vibrations of the shifting ice into his boots and the soles of his feet; a reminder that glaciers are in constant flow. Rockfall noise came suddenly from the left and they swung headlight beams in that direction, and listened, motionless. The cracking and tumbling noise Dopplered away from them as the falling rock passed harmlessly to the side and cascaded downslope. Esmond exhaled; the condensation plume hung in the still air like a wraith around his head.

"A lot of activity for so early in the day. We'll need to be extra sharp on rockfall duty," he said as Gianna stepped next to him.

After another hour of zig-zagging upward — using the French technique to keep all points of the crampons engaged in the ice — they stopped. The glacier angled up even steeper, here. The sky was light enough to reveal more details of the route and Esmond puzzled at a mass of man-sized ice chunks blocking their path.

He looked upslope and startled, "What the hell?"

Klickitat, which in current season should be a lumpy, more or less contiguous, undulating surface, was a hacked-up mess. Instead of finding a handful of narrow crevasses with good, solid snow bridges, they were confronted with numerous wide cracks. Horizontal crevasses split wide, grinning at them with dark, hungry mouths. And there were no snow paths across. Surprisingly, there were also vertical slots, which intersected the horizontal ones at right-angles like carved-up brownies in a pan — except these rectangular ice chunks were SUV, boxcar, and house-sized blocks. And each of the teetering seracs looked ready to topple and crush them under thousands of tons of ice.

The wreckage of one of the seracs spilled downslope to where Esmond's boots had stopped moments earlier. It was only one of the small ones, but it would have wiped them both out. Everything looked melted. Unstable. Dangerous. Like a shattered plate-glass window.

"Didn't you go look at the glacier last night?" asked Gianna.

"Yes. But the ridge obscured this lower portion. The top looked fine."

Esmond got the monocular out of his pack and trained the optics along Battlement Ridge, up to The Castle, and along the upper reaches of the glacier.

"I don't understand," he exclaimed, and pulled the eyepiece away. "From the base of The Castle down, the glacier is chopped to hell. It's pulled away from the ridge and there's a moat running all the way up the northeast side. There's been lots of rock and icefall. Looks like a late August melt-out on the bottom, but the top is perfect."

Under their feet the glacier groaned again, then stilled.

"What do we do?" asked Gianna.

"We could climb in the moat to The Castle base and then hop onto better ice up there, but we didn't really prep for a lot of rock, and this stuff crumbles like stale biscotti. It is the worst choss-rock shit to hang your life on. Plus, I don't want to be climbing up under that ridge getting bombed from above. I say we pull the plug on this."

A *clack* echoed off the ridge wall and they watched a fridge-sized rock fall and shatter into smaller projectiles that bounced and tumbled downslope, like a mountainous bowling alley. Overhead, a mass of dark clouds was forming over The Castle. A warm, sickly, sulfur-laden breeze blew down from above. The rotten-egg stench made them gag.

Boom!

A rock slab the size of a luxury-yacht began sliding off Battlement Ridge, directly across from them. Instinctively, Esmond and Gianna began a hasty retreat backwards, across and away to the southwest side of the glacier. In slow motion, the massive basalt formation sailed down into the glacier and exploded.

They retreated faster.

Chunks of rock and ice burst upward and began raining down.

They turned and ran.

The shape of the fall line saved them. The angle was steeper on the opposite side, and gravity pulled the cascading shattering mass in that direction. They were just high enough that the blast fragments passed downslope of them. The impact zone pushed a tsunami of snow, ice, and rock in a sweeping wave downhill. The avalanche roared like a jet fighter with full afterburners on. Kicking up a roiling, misty cloud, it crashed all the way across the glacier below them. Reverberations bounded off of the ridge.

The path they had travelled was buried.

They stood, unmoving, and watched. The noise faded. The last reflecting echoes whispered to quiet. Then they both started talking at once. Esmond looked up, for any sign of more falling objects. He stiffened and hushed Gianna.

The clouds above The Castle had started a slow rotation: the beginnings of a vortex, like just before a tornado.

And something was walking downhill.

Gianna felt her partner go rigid as he implored her to be silent. She looked up and saw the odd rotating mass of clouds, which she thought were the wind effects of the massive avalanche that had nearly killed them. Esmond was silent. She could see from behind that he faced a point lower than the vortex.

Then she saw where he was looking.

A man seemed to be hopping or floating — not walking — towards them. A red-helmeted person with a black hang glider. *No. That doesn't make sense.*

Sometimes people did launch hang gliders off of mountaintops, but not at dawn and not down icefalls or avalanches.

"Jesus Christ!" said Esmond.

Shaking, he dropped the monocular. He fumbled with his harness, then untied the rope, disconnecting their shared bond. He unbuckled and dropped his pack and turned to her.

"Go down now."

"What is it?" she implored, confused.

A deafening roar sounded, like the screeching of train brakes.

"Go down *now*," he commanded.

Gianna was still trying to process everything when Esmond began to move up at an angle, toward the person descending. Gianna picked up the monocular, and focused it. Her confusion intensified and then yielded to a growing sense of dread. The shape, which she thought was a man, flexed and extended a pair of wings from impossibly broad shoulders. She screamed.

Esmond strode towards it, wielding both ice axes. He paused, turned, and shouted at her. He was thirty yards away, but she saw the urgency in his posture.

"GO!" he yelled.

She raised the monocular again. She couldn't find the creature, and pulled away the lens to scan with her naked eyes. Her peripheral vision flashed a warning and she pivoted to see it gliding and landing less than a hundred yards from Esmond.

It bellowed again, and Esmond froze mid-stride. He seemed stuck. Gianna looked through the monocular. The red 'helmet' was a mass of writhing snakes. Below that flashed red luminescent eyes, and a long, black tongue snaked out of a dark, fanged maw. She felt a dark malevolent gaze wash over her, and a chill penetrated deep into the marrow of her bones.

As it hopped closer, she saw Esmond still hadn't moved. Time slowed.

Gianna's wrists, neck, and ring finger burned. A tingling, buzzing warmth built and spread, like the feeling returning to an oxygen-starved limb.

Esmond toppled forward, but caught the fall by landing on his left foot and slamming both axes into the ice. Right knee down, he looked like an Arthurian Knight as he pushed down on the ice tools and slowly rose. He stepped towards the creature.

This is not real. It can't be real. Gianna stood frozen, like an insect trapped and fossilized in amber, even though her heart hammered with surging adrenalin. The primal emotional states, fight and flight, battled for control and she was paralyzed until one emerged as the victor.

He took another step forward and raised the axes over his head.

Wings flared on the creature of Greek nightmares as it closed in on Esmond.

Move or die, Gianna's feral side screamed at her.

The Gorgon was now less than twenty yards from Esmond.

Her heart — *her love* — shattered the incapacitating fear, and she charged.

In a full crampon-biting ice sprint, Gianna ran towards them, and saw the monster's eyes glowing brighter. A beam of crimson light shot out and enveloped Esmond. It flared and then warped into shimmering mirage lines, blocking her sight.

When the distortion phased away, she saw an ice sculpture. A frozen mountaineer: ice axes raised: one foot lifted. *Esmond!*

The Gorgon looked at Gianna and stomped towards her. Raising its wings and roaring, it backhanded the Esmond ice statue, which shattered.

Gianna screamed in primal rage. The monster smiled and its long, black tongue licked white fangs.

The shimmering began again. Gianna could see it beginning to project from the Gorgon's eyes. Her ice axe, gripped in gloveless hands, glowed white-hot in front of her. She was distracted from the monster by the shaft of the axe. Metal swirled and flowed in eddies and micro-currents. Small mercurial streams flowed onto Gianna's hands, where they branched and traced spider-web lines to her ring, bracelet, and watch.

Gianna's long black dreadlocks bobbed in the breeze from the cloud vortex. The Gorgon hesitated; the red pit-vipers snapped, hissed, coiled, and retreated.

The Gorgon gaze shot out, and Gianna could see nothing beyond her raised arms — which were now flowing with criss-crossing silvery lines, extending up over her forearms, moving higher, towards her torso and neck. She felt warm. Heightened. Aware. And alive.

Above, the vortex spun faster. Lightning flashed.

The distortion vanished.

Gianna was stunned —

— but then reared back with both arms, and drove the spike of the glowing axe deep into the creature's right side.

The Gorgon screamed. Blood sprayed over Gianna from the chest wound as it stumbled backwards.

It flew. Crashed. Flew again. And then it retreated in short uphill hops toward The Castle, bellowing.

In cold fury, Gianna pursued close on the hooves of the Gorgon.

Reaching The Castle, it turned and roared at her, then limped into a black, shimmering portal, and vanished.

Gianna did not hesitate; she held aloft her axe — now shining as bright as a star — and dove into the black void; into the depths beneath The Castle. Seeking revenge.

PROTECTORS

PROLOGUE

March 20th , 1975

At 10:45 PM, a US Air Force C-141 Starlifter (Military Air Command flight #40461) neared the end of its 20-hour flight from the Philippines to McChord Air Force Base, in Washington State. During its long journey it had stops in Okinawa and Japan, where some additional cargo — securely locked — was loaded. MAC flight #40461 was still over the Pacific Ocean when Air Traffic Control (ATC) in Seattle instructed the C-141, a four jet-engine strategic transport capable of carrying almost one hundred thousand pounds of cargo, to descend from its cruising altitude of 37,000 ft, down to 15,000 ft.

At 11PM, the C-141 crossed the coastline and entered the rugged, mountainous Olympic Peninsula amid stormy conditions. Confusing the C-141 with a different military flight of A6 Intruders over Puget Sound, ATC mistakenly issued a descend to 5,000 ft. Five minutes later, the C-141 — containing 16 crew and passengers — slammed into the steep sides of a 7,399 ft jagged peak.

The search and rescue teams struggled with the remote nature of the mountain, and were held off by the storms and avalanches. What the helicopters could see from the air during brief breaks in the weather dashed any hope of survivors. Debris was scattered over a wide area, and the wrecked fuselage had wedged, or perhaps fused, into a natural vertical slot in the craggy, unnamed mountain.

The mission changed from search and rescue to recovery.

No one survived. It took almost three months to recover the remains of the sixteen bodies.

May 4th, 2012

Takeo Kita finished stuffing his mountaineering pack at the trailhead, and remembered to hang the America the Beautiful National Park pass from the rear-view mirror of his Jeep. Still fighting off the idea that he had forgotten something, he braced the pack on the bumper of the vehicle. Easing into the straps, he stood upright and groaned at the weight.

A light pack is critical for moving up steep terrain, but the right equipment is critical for survival. These competing principles torture climbers. *What if I need that? What if I exhaust myself, or fall from too much weight?*

In Tak's case, a solo, four-day climbing trek in the snowy mountains and untamed wilderness of the Olympic Peninsula was something to be prepared for — but he told himself: *don't pack more crap than you can carry.* Takeo had been down the too-much-mass path before. It sucked. Having forgone the kitchen-sink this time, he still felt he still had too much weight. He had also probably forgotten something, but wasn't going to add a single gram to his back at this point. *I never seem to be able to find the right balance.*

Tak checked his watch, turned on his GPS unit, and started along the Upper Dungeness Trail (trail #833.2). His destination today was Home Lake, nestled up at 5,000 ft and not too far from Constance Pass. He would set base camp there to serve as a launching point for some challenging climbs in the immediate region. Warrior Peak, C-141, and Mount Constance were all on the agenda, conditions permitting.

The distance to Home Lake was just over 14 miles. For the first few miles, Takeo enjoyed the solitude and the relative ease of the undulating path winding alongside the roaring Dungeness River. The trail crossed the river in a few places by means of a single, peeled log with a nailed-on wooden rail perched on one side. One of the log crossings, slick from mist and algae, almost dumped him 20 feet down onto the rocks and rushing water below, when the tread of his boot slipped. This wrenched a muscle in Takeo's lower back and he swore in pain.

He passed Camp Handy, a lean-to structure by the water, and a mile or so later the trail went steeply uphill. The pack got heavier, his back hurt, and the joy of the start of a new adventure began to dissipate. *It's all part of the experience,* he thought. Pain and suffering. He trudged upwards and a few miles later entered Boulder Shelter, a small flat area nestled in a cirque — a natural amphitheater bowl — in the mountain ridge. A small creek funneled down through it and eventually joined the Dungeness River far below.

Boulder Shelter marked a confluence of trails, and contained a roofed three-sided wooden shack, about the size of a small hotel room. It was a good camp spot and Tak had stayed here before. Signposts pointed out the trails to Marmot Pass, Charlia Lakes, and Home Lake. The car- and truck-sized lichen-covered boulders scattered about had tumbled down centuries ago from the mountain peak looming above.

Takeo decided on a ten-minute break and was glad to slide the pack down off his back, which was complaining about the weight and the near fall. He glanced up. The peak looming above him didn't have an official name. Lacking in aesthetic beauty and being of no real interest to climbers, it bore a simple label on his topographical map: *6599,* indicating the altitude of its summit.

He mused about the upcoming days as he sat on a rock and hydrated. There were several peaks along the Inner Constance ridge that he had eyed for climbing. The ridge was directly above him but he couldn't yet see any of the peaks that interested him. One of them, C-141, used to be known as Constance Lookout, because of the fire-watch platform that had once been there. People had ignored it or hadn't called it anything at all.

That had been true until that crash in 1975. Now people knew it as C-141 — a memorial to the fallen.

Break over, Takeo resumed his trek and left Boulder Shelter via the trail marked Home Lake. He wasn't sure why it was called that; it was nowhere near home for anyone. He passed underneath Warrior Peak and paused to study its twin-tower summit.

Continuing on, the trail traversed the steep western side of the Inner Constance ridge, descended a little ways into a narrow valley and then crossed for the final switchbacks up to the lake. He stopped at a set of fresh animal tracks in the snow, squatting to inspect them. Definitely cougar; and probably less than an hour old, judging by the unmelted ice-crystal rim of the print in the warm sun.

He grunted as he rose from his squat, and surveyed in the direction the tracks led. He didn't see anything. Tak rotated 360 degrees to scan around him. Nothing.

He continued uphill. The first day, with a full pack, was always the worst part of the trip. Well, that and the final exhausting slog back out to the trailhead when all the climbing was done.

Arriving at Home Lake, he dropped the heavy pack and hunted around for a good camp spot. The weight off his back and shoulders made him feel buoyant and lighter than normal. The trip up had taken eight hours and his body was worn out. Now that he had stopped the masochistic upward trek, Tak's body was filling him in on details: sore spots, kinked muscles, and aching bones and joints that let him know that his cessation of abuse was welcomed. It was kind of like when you finished running a marathon or stopped hitting yourself with a hammer. It just felt good.

Takeo had the lake to himself, as he had hoped. He busied himself and soon had the lightweight tent up. He stuffed his sleeping bag, food, and other soft gear inside. The sun was high in the azure sky and there were no clouds. He found a nice rock and stretched out in the sun. Munching on a sandwich he looked across the narrow valley at C-141. Such an awful tragedy. The plane had flown right into the notch he was staring at. Tak tried to imagine it. A huge cargo jet plowing into that peak at several hundred miles per hour.

He'd heard from other climbers that pieces of the aircraft or cargo still turned up at times.

Tak sighed and continued to gaze.

Like most peaks in this area, it rose quickly from the valley. The lower slopes were currently encased in shadows, which would rise and deepen quickly with the coming sunset. The absence of trees in wide patches on the snowy low slopes spoke to the frequency of avalanches.

Tak's gaze moved up the mountain to the summit. The sun behind him reflected harshly off the ice and snow, and he put his sunglasses on. The upper mountain was pregnant with piled snow.

A cool breeze sighed through the conifers surrounding the small lake. The smell of pine and the warmth of the sun made Takeo sleepy, and he drifted off right there, like a cougar napping on a warm rock after a meal. His eyelids and lips twitched as he fell into rapid-eye-movement sleep. Vivid dreams took over.

A roar woke him.

A jet engine screamed in the valley. Tak sat bolt upright. The confusion of sleep, and dreams of mountain lions, vanished. His eyes focused in the direction of the noise and saw the leading edge and plumes of an avalanche crashing down C-141. He jumped up on the rock upon which he'd been dozing. From the primal recesses of his brain came fear.

Wide awake now, the rational side of his brain saw that he was in no danger. His campsite was several hundred feet above the narrow floor of the valley. Even a massive tsunami crashing below could not reach him. Had the avalanche crashed earlier, while Tak was crossing down there, it would have been a different story.

But from where he was, he had a perfectly safe, surround-sound, big-screen, private showing of the fast-moving wave of death. Avalanches are beautifully terrifying to watch. As the roaring subsided, and the echoes from the ridge walls faded, a white mist hung above the valley. And as it settled, the extent of the slide became apparent. A football-field sized swath, several feet thick, had come loose.

Takeo retrieved his binoculars to examine it. Inspecting, he could see the sharp step-off line where the slab had fractured. The line cut about three or four feet deep, then extended about fifty yards across the face. The release had occurred about halfway up the mountain.

Tak continued scrutinizing. Many avalanches were human triggered. He searched for signs of humans or gear. If people had been caught, Tak might be the only person capable of helping. He pulled the binoculars away from his face and studied. Putting the binoculars to his eyes again, he spotted a curious object, or objects, in the snow.

Damn! That's a tent and gear. Someone got slammed. I need to go help.

Tak stuffed what he thought he might need into his pack: first aid kit, extra clothing, headlamp, water, and emergency beacon. Shaking from adrenalin, he checked his watch to verify the daylight he thought he had left, and started the stopwatch. He slung on the pack.

He scanned with his binoculars again and breathed slowly to calm his tremors. His heart hammered as he surveyed the slope across the valley. He spotted a rectangle and flapping bright red and white material. A tent or a flag. No sign of people, nor any motion.

The snow dampened all sound. Tak heard his pulse pounding.

He knelt to strap on his crampons, then stood, grabbed his ice axe and helmet, and strode down the trail. Moving downhill with a light load, he arrived at the avalanche quickly. He rechecked his watch; 1 min 30 seconds since the slide. *Max survival time for a buried victim is 5 minutes.*

He entered the debris field and began looking for clothing, gear, or limbs sticking up from the jumbled, solidified white mess. He saw nothing and moved upslope, faster once beyond the obstacle course of snow and ice blocks.

The exposed snow layer underneath the slide, felt stable under his crampons. But he had to be wary of more slides. Sprinting uphill, heart feeling like it would burst, he spied the objects.

He paused to allow his body to recover and to reassess the risk.

Part of the slope on this face had thundered down in a big avalanche, probably due to warming after the recent storm. This checked a pretty obvious red flag on the risk assessment scoresheet. He could see the book from the avalanche safety course as if it were in front of him.

Are there signs of recent avalanches in the area? And are conditions right for more?

Yes. And yes.

If yes to both, turn around.

The proper advice. But what if someone is buried, and you are their only hope? Tak couldn't turn around. There was something human-made there, he had no doubt. But was there a person or people? He checked his watch. Three minutes since the avalanche. He had to find out.

He took a direct line to the objects, which were about a third the way up the face. The slope under his feet was at a 45- or 50-degree angle, and then kicked up steeper toward the summit. Nervous energy drove him; he took large lungfuls of air and his thighs burned in pain from the effort. *Not much further to go.*

About ten yards from his destination, he slowed and scoured the surface for any sign of a person. The objects resolved themselves. What he had thought was a tent turned out to be a cloth rectangle; some kind of flag. The other object was a wooden crate about four feet in length, a foot wide, and a foot deep. Both looked old and worn.

Takeo stopped to allow his lungs and heart a chance to recover.

The flag had a red circle in the center, with white and red rays extending out. The Rising Sun of the Imperial Japanese Army; a pre-1945 version, and it looked authentic. He moved beside the wooden crate and knelt down. The box — dense, old, rich oak — was well constructed but had been through hell. It had scorch marks, divots, and a few chunks missing. Tak brushed snow off and saw Kanji adorning the edge of one surface. The lettering was faded and missing in places.

Takeo stood and examined the surrounding snow, trying to puzzle out what this box and flag were doing here. They were certainly not anything climbers would be hauling around. He took some photos with his smartphone and then stomped around the area, trying to see if there was anything else, and looking for any signs of humans. Nothing.

Deciding that remaining here any longer simply increased his risk, Tak looked for the best way to get the box and flag back to camp. He stuffed the flag in his pack. He tested the weight of the box and found that it approximated one-half of the full load he had carried up to Home Lake. He sat down on the snow, and braced the box across his hips at a 90-degree angle. Holding onto it with one arm, and wielding the ice-axe with the other, he started butt sliding. Much faster than the lung-busting ascent to get up there, the glissade down plopped him at the edge of the avalanche runout below. *Sometimes flying by the seat of your pants is the only way*.

For the uphill part, he carried the box in the crooks of his elbows, resting at intervals. Thirty minutes later he lugged it into camp and set it down. The sun was gone from the tips of the peaks across the valley. He had an hour and change until darkness. He prepped dinner, ate, and stared at the oak box. Curiosity soon won out and he began examining the surface. Tak couldn't decipher the Kanji. It was too scratched out, but he saw it was an old font.

His fingers explored the weathered surface. There were no joints, nails, or fasteners. At one time, he thought, this had been a polished-smooth surface showing rich woodgrain. He brushed dirt off of one end and saw the flush-peg construction. *What is this?*

The oak on this box was carefully shaped to fit together like a puzzle. This particular puzzle had been through a lot but Takeo was certain it was built by a *sashimono-shi,* an artisan of intricate wooden furniture. The craft dated back more than a thousand years and had survived into modern times because it was simply amazing: no glue, nails, screws, or power tools.

Tak explored further. He closed his eyes and let all ten fingertips slide over the oak. *Yes, you are a puzzle,* he thought. He moved each hand to opposite ends of the box and pressed into specific pegs. There was a *click*, and then a crease split along the long axis and a gap appeared. Tak removed the lid and peered in.

A katana lay inside.

He closed his hands around the scabbard, and closed his eyes.

Tak slept poorly. He rocked awake when winds gusted or hail slammed into the tent. The forecast had indicated calm, but sometimes storm bands formed from nowhere in the Olympics. Sometimes the clouds didn't listen to the forecast.

And it was hitting pretty hard.

When he did doze off again, his mind filled with jarring, colorful images. He spoke with the images. Imploring. Trying to understand. He felt a longing to answer a far-off call. *I must return. Honor. Duty.*

Panting, he sat bolt upright, and tried to parse the images while they were still in his brain. He checked his surroundings. *Those were intense dreams*, he thought. Outside, the storm continued its assault, and Takeo flicked on his headlight. 3 AM: alpine start time, but the storm was too severe to think about climbing, so he snuggled deeper into the bag and closed his eyes.

In his dreams he chased something. There were crowds. Screaming.

When he woke up again at 6 AM, he was covered in sweat. The tent fluttered from the winds of the storm that wasn't showing any signs of fading. Climbing was pretty much out of the question, at least for today. Even if the storm stopped now, there wouldn't be enough time to accomplish even one of his goals, and the snow dump changed the avalanche risk in the wrong direction. Damn it.

He unzipped a small section of the tent to peer outside. His headlight picked up snow blowing horizontally in the dark dawn. He shrugged, zipped the tent closed, and readjusted his position in the sleeping bag. He soon fell asleep in the swaying tent.

He dreamt of a woman in a small shop in a downstairs corridor, in Pike Place Market in Seattle. He had been there before and had spoken with her in Japanese. She knows history and culture. She will know what the sword means. I must see her now.

At 8 AM he decided it was time to get up. He puzzled at the emotions and images of his dreams. He looked at the sword. *Funny, I don't remember bringing the sword into the tent.*

He layered up and went outside to pee. Returning, he crouched by the tent, sheltered against the wind, and lit the stove. He crawled back into the tent, with only his head sticking out, and tended to the pot as it boiled.

He prepped breakfast, then considered his next steps as he slurped warm cinnamon oatmeal and sipped hot coffee. The storm cleared.

He needed to see the Japanese woman in Pike Place Market.

Urgently.

Takeo packed his gear. He lashed the wooden box to the pack and bemoaned the excess weight. *Well at least its all downhill*, he thought and plunged down the snow-filled trail.

Six hours later Tak arrived at his Jeep. He carefully removed and stored the sword, and then flung his pack in the back. He sat down in the driver's seat and groaned as he pulled off his boots and slipped sneakers onto his sore feet.

He started the engine, and bumped down the single lane packed-dirt and gravel Forest Service road leaving a plume of dust in his wake. He turned right on Highway 101. His homeward journey took him on Highway 104, across the Hood Canal Bridge, onto Highway 3, and then into Poulsbo.

It was twilight by the time Tak parked the Jeep and carried the sword up to his apartment. He showered, put a pot of chili on the stove, and called his girlfriend.

"Hi Hon. I'm off the mountain early."

"Everything ok?" she asked. There was background noise and laughter.

"Yes. Just bad weather. I'm going to eat and go to bed. Want to get together tomorrow night?"

"Sure. That'd be great," she replied. "Sorry about the noise. It's girls' night out tonight."

"No worries. I forgot you were going out," he said, and then paused. "I found something that belongs to someone and I need to go into Seattle tomorrow. I'll be back in the afternoon."

"Ok Tak, but it'll be really crowded, the Japanese national team is playing an exhibition game against the Mariners," she said. "Be safe. I'll call you tomorrow and we'll make dinner plans. Cool?"

"Sounds great. Say hi to the girls for me. Love you, Jules."

"Will do. Glad you're back safely. Love you too Tak. See ya."

Tak transferred the chili to a bowl, added some shredded cheddar cheese and sour cream, and sat down at the dining room table. He ravenously attacked the chili, periodically glancing at the sword propped in the corner. He got up to get a second helping of chili. On the way back to the table, his eyes lingered on the sword. *Where did you come from? And who do you belong to?*

❖

Tak slept deeply and in the morning drove to the Bainbridge Island ferry terminal, where he parked and then walked on to the 7:55 am boat to Seattle. He went to the upper deck and gazed out across Puget Sound. The rising sun was well above the horizon and the flickering sunlight danced on the emerald water, mesmerizing Takeo. He tried to recall the vivid dreams from last night. The images escaped him, but he felt a strong sense of duty, and a compulsion to be in Pike Place Public Market this morning. *But why?*

He found a remote spot on the deck and sat down cross-legged. Tak removed his pack and unstrapped the cloth wrapped sword, which he laid across his lap. He slid back the end of the cloth and examined the intricacies of the black *ito* wrapping on the hilt. Running his fingers over it, he was surprised to find it warm. Gripping the hilt firmly in his right hand, Tak closed his eyes: images filled his mind. He saw a thousand battles through a warrior's eyes. A warrior who protected vulnerable citizens and vanquished evil.

The ferry bumped into the slip at Coleman dock startling Tak from his reverie. He looked at his watch and discovered that he had been dozing for 30 minutes. Securing the sword to the pack, and making sure it was covered, Tak exited the ferry and passed through the terminal building. He walked on the elevated walkway above Marion Street and then took a left at 1st Avenue and headed uphill to Pike Place Public Market.

Takeo felt a little weird walking along with a katana on his back. It was wrapped in black cloth so he probably only looked strange, and not necessarily dangerous. He imagined he could explain he was getting an antique appraised if the Seattle Police stopped him, but it was better to be discreet. Now, if he were walking along 3rd Avenue — with its shouting masses of schizophrenic methheads leaping on passersby and pissing on bus stops — he could probably swing the sword in large circles over his head, reciting Biblical verses, and no one would notice.

He ducked into a covered tunnel in the maze that made up the extended market. Pushing through throngs of tourists, he looked for the shop he remembered from his dreams, which was tucked away from the main corridor. The metal chime above the door announced his presence when he walked in.

From behind a large glass display case a tiny, wizened Japanese woman bowed to him.

"Welcome, Takeo-san," she said in Japanese.

He bowed. And then froze. *How did she know my name? I've been here before, but how could she remember my name?* Tak looked around the curiosity shop. There were items packed into every corner: brightly colored kimonos, gold-joined *Kintsugi* pottery, ceramic tea pots, mini-*wakizashi* letter openers, painted silk scrolls, hand-carved wood *netsuke*, and intricate wood-block ink prints. It reminded him of the Tokyo flea markets. Every surface and wall of the small shop had been put to good use. Although dense, there was a precise order to things.

"May I see the sword?" she asked.

"Huh?"

"The sword. You brought it here for me to examine, yes?" she inquired, and trotted around the counter on tiny feet.

"Um, yes. I did," he answered, and then looked over his shoulder at the exit.

"It's fine. You are safe," she said, and stepped toward him with arms extended and both palms facing up. "Now let's see the blade."

Tak placed the sheathed weapon onto her upturned hands. She turned and put it on the display counter. She unwrapped the black cloth carefully, turned on a gooseneck lamp, and adjusted her glasses. She peered closely at the hilt, and then withdrew the blade six inches from the scabbard.

She gasped, re-sheathed the blade, and left it on the display case. She sat down on a stool and reached for her cup of tea with a shaky hand. Tak looked at the sword on the counter and then his gaze was caught by a bright yellow-lettered Japanese wanted poster hanging in the background. It advertised a reward for information leading to the arrest of Yuji Fimori, the last remaining fugitive from the 1995 sarin nerve gas attack on the Tokyo subway system, conducted by the death cult, Aum Shinrikyo.

The sound of the tea cup being placed on its saucer brought his eyes back to the old woman.

"This is the Honjō Masamune," she said, and then gestured for Takeo to sit. "The Honjō Masamune is the most famous blade in all of Japan. It was forged in the 14th century by Gorō Nyūdō Masamune, the greatest Japanese swordsmith to ever live. It is said that the edges of his swords are only one molecule thick and will cut anything. This sword is his most important work and has been missing since 1945; stolen by Americans after they bombed us and made us surrender our swords. It is a national treasure that has long been searched for."

Takeo was going to interrupt to ask a question but was silenced by the old woman as she cleared her throat.

"In legend, Masamune once had a contest with his finest pupil, Muramasa. They took their best blades into the forest to decide whose was best. Muramasa put his sword in a brook with the sharp edge pointed upstream. It cut everything that came close. Leaves were split in half. Fishes swimming along were carved up as if by a master sushi chef."

"Masamune nodded at the impressive blade his pupil had created, and placed his own sword in the water. Leaves floating downstream were split in the same way as with Muramasa's blade, but no fish died. No fish were even cut. Nothing happened to them. Muramasa smiled and proclaimed his blade better. But a monk who had watched the whole affair had a different interpretation. Masamune's blade was superior, because it didn't kill the innocent.

Muramasa's blade was an indiscriminate killing machine. It needed blood every time it was drawn," she concluded.

Takeo went to the display case and studied the sheathed weapon. He rolled it over in his hands.

"It's hard to believe that this is the actual sword," he said.

"How did you come across this weapon?" she asked.

Takeo told her the story as she poured more tea for them both. When he was finished she was silent for a while and then locked eyes with Takeo.

"It has chosen you," she said. "This sword can only be used for good. You must listen to the dreams it gives you, because it speaks the truth."

"I don't understand."

"The Honjō Masamune seeks a wielder who is pure, for its mission of justice. The sword has had many bearers. If you are honest, it will stay by your side for life and will avenge your death. But it will leave one who is dishonest or who seeks to use the weapon for personal gain or ill purpose. The sword will always show you the true path. You must not fight it. You have been chosen."

"But…"

"Get used to it," she said, cutting him off.

Tak stood, retrieved the sword, and came back to his seat. He placed his hand on the hilt and felt a vibration; a tiny, almost imperceptible tingling in his right hand.

Behind them, the door chimes tinkled and a middle-aged Japanese man with a backpack stepped onto the creaking wood floor. The old woman rose and issued a traditional greeting.

The man turned, bowed, and smiled. He had a pistol pointed at them.

"Yuji Fimori!" gasped the old woman.

"You remember me. Now it's time to forget. There's nothing you can do to stop me this time," said the man in Japanese.

The sword flashed out as Yuji fired. Takeo saw a hollow-point bullet frozen in time. Then the Honjō Masamune split the projectile, and fragments impacted the wall behind.

Yuji's eyes grew round in surprise. Tak took a step toward him and he fled the store. Tak turned and checked on the old woman. She was uninjured

"You must stop him," she said, clutching her chest. "He has nerve gas and will kill everyone."

Tak sheathed the weapon and sprinted out the door.

Outside the shop he searched to see which direction Yuji had fled. He knew he must stop the man before many people died. He heard a crash and saw a fruit stand topple over. Running in that direction, he heard yelling, and then saw a disturbance up ahead, moving through Pike Street like a salmon against the current. The buzzing energy in the hilt of the sheathed sword intensified in his palm.

He heard screaming, and felt a disorienting moment of déjà vu. People were backing away from the gun-wielding Yuji as he shoved his way through the crowds. He took a right turn at 3rd Avenue and headed south.

Tak followed at a full sprint. The streets were crowded and waves of pedestrians were headed south. He saw people in baseball jerseys, and a poster in Japanese and English advertising the Samurai vs. Mariners game.

His heart hammered in his chest. Yuji was heading for the dense throngs clustering around the stadium. It was unlikely that he would get through security, but he didn't need to. Just releasing the nerve agent among the crowded street parties and plazas outside the stadium would result in the deaths of thousands. He must be stopped.

Tak gained ground, and Yuji took a right on James Street, near the courthouse. Tak rounded the corner, and the sword flashed up and intercepted a bullet before he had even heard the gunshot. He slid to a stop. His left shoulder burned and a small flow of blood ran down his arm. *It must be a bullet fragment.*

Several people were screaming in fear and had ducked away from the sidewalk to shelter behind parked cars. Tak scanned around. Yuji emerged from concealment in the alley, ran across the street, and went around the corner at 2nd Street, still headed to the stadiums.

Tak followed. The blade had saved him twice. The first could have been random chance, but the second instance of the blade splitting a bullet put the Honjō Masamune beyond anything rational or possible.

Tak flew around the corner at 2nd and saw Yuji duck down Yesler Way. Tak was gaining, and around the next corner he saw Yuji turn into the crowded, noisy pedestrian thoroughfare of Occidental Avenue.

They were in Pioneer Square; only a few blocks from the stadium. Revelers chanted and danced along the streets, music boomed, and the smells of burgers, sausage, beer, and cannabis filled the air.

Crossing Washington Street, Yuji stumbled to avoid a car. Tak gained further.

"Stop!" he yelled in Japanese as he caught up with Yuji at Occidental Square, at the Fallen Firefighters Memorial. Yuji dove and hid behind one of the tumbled concrete blocks next to a life-sized metal statue of a gas-masked firefighter. Takeo used a line of trees flanking the redbrick square to advance to within 20 yards. Yuji fired his gun, and the round impacted the tree in front of Takeo.

The people packing the square veered away from the memorial at the sound of gunfire, and silence descended on the crowd.

"Step closer and everyone dies," yelled Yuji in Japanese.

Some in the crowd stopped talking and extracted smartphones to video the street performance of two shouting Japanese men; an older one with a gun versus a younger one with a sword.

Others dialed 911.

Takeo peered around the tree and saw that Yuji was pointing a semi-automatic pistol at him with his right hand, and holding up a black cylinder in his left. The cylinder had a black coiled wire emerging from the bottom, and a red button on the top. Yuji's thumb was resting on the button. The wire disappeared up his sleeve.

"You know I have nerve gas. Right, asshole?" shouted Yuji. "I release this button, and the cylinders on my back explode; the gas goes everywhere. Ten kilograms of pure VX. Much more potent than sarin. Primed for wide dispersal. Enough to kill twenty thousand."

Some in the crowd fled.

"OK. I won't step any closer," responded Tak, surveying his surrounding to estimate distance and obstacles. He switched the Honjō Masamune to a single grip in his right hand. He calculated that he had one chance, which depended upon several factors.

First: Yuji had a dead-man's switch leading to the pack. As long as he held the button down, the device would not go off.

Second: when surprised, many people clamp down.

Third: he knew via the sword that Yuji was about to release his thumb.

A plan emerged: a powerful and precise *kote* strike, to sever the wrist.

And then time slowed. The fluttering leaves on the deciduous tree above Tak stilled, and birds froze in flight. His heart rate slowed. He dove forward to roll over his right shoulder, and the sword blurred through a 360-degree, low, flat arc just above the red brick pavement. Tak popped up and landed in a solid stance to the side of Yuji with a double-hand grip on the hilt. And as the blade flashed down, Tak yelled, "Kote!"

Time shifted back to normal speed and Tak heard people screaming. He looked down and saw both of Yuji's severed hands on the pavement. There was a gun gripped in the right hand; the trigger-cylinder was clenched in the left. There had been no explosion.

The thumb was only now relaxing off the red button, but the cut wires had rendered the trigger harmless.

Yuji was moaning on the pavement and losing blood. Tak removed his shirt and used the sword to cut long strips, and applied these as tourniquets to Yuji's wrist stumps. Gingerly, Tak removed the pack full of nerve gas and leaned it against one of the gas-masked firefighter statues.

He stepped back and took in the full memorial. A wave of solemnity and gratitude washed over him as powerfully as when he had first visited the memorial years ago.

Tak saw shocked expressions on the nearby onlookers and many were still filming, as he cleaned and sheathed the sword. Police and paramedics arrived and began attending to Yuji.

"Hey buddy, you ok?" one of the paramedics asked Tak. "You're bleeding."

"Yeah. I'm ok. Grazed, but I'm ok."

❖

Six hours later, Tak emerged from the Seattle Police Department headquarters with his sword secured to his back. The SPD had seen video footage and the bomb squad had transferred Yuji's backpack to the US Army. They were going to charge him with a list of crimes, but then two people from the US State Department had visited. Soon after, the police had let him go.

The videos of the incident that had been uploaded to YouTube, Instagram, Facebook, and Snapchat had been seen in Japan and across the US. The scene of Tak's spectacular disarming and capture of the most wanted man in Japan had spread quickly and widely.

The State Department folks said he was a hero in both countries, but advised him to keep a low profile. Both Prime Minister Yoshihiko Noda and President Barack Obama wanted to meet him, and the State Department would be in touch soon. *Here's the number for anything you might need.*

Tak walked in the late afternoon sunshine, heading downhill on Columbia Street towards Coleman dock. Thirty minutes later, he stood along a railing on the upper deck of the ferry MV Puyallup as it sailed away from the dock to cross Puget Sound towards the setting sun.

SIGNALS

In the soil of fear are planted the seeds of deception.

Portage Glacier Highway, Alaska, Oct 30 2021

A sun-bleached blue Chevy, towing an equally aged U-Haul trailer, pulled up to the ticket booth for the Anton Anderson Memorial Tunnel. *I can't wait for this shit to burn*, thought the sole passenger licking his dry lips underneath a black balaclava. He pulled down the brim of his black Raiders hat, slouched low in his seat, and looked sideways at the driver, who wore mirrored sunglasses and a camouflage neckerchief pulled up over his face.

The driver paid in cash and then pulled forward. A gate closed behind them, signaling the end of traffic for this run through the tunnel. The Chevy rumbled to the end of the queue in the staging area and stopped. The driver yawned and stretched his large frame, and the old springs in the car seat creaked in protest. The interior of the car had a musty smell of ash and from the splits in the black vinyl upholstery spilled yellow crumbly foam. The driver pulled off his neckerchief, revealing a short, red Balbo beard and a neck tattoo of Poseidon wielding a trident. A flowing mane of red hair brushed across his large shoulders and his neck muscles bulged as he turned his square head to look at the passenger. When he smiled dimples deepened in his ruddy cheeks.

"Wipe the fucking grin," said Raider-cap.

A frown creased the driver's forehead. He sat forward, squeezing the steering wheel with large, callused hands, and then shrugged. "Relax, man – we're here," he said.

Raider-cap pulled his balaclava down and lit a cigarette. He took a drag, and then flicked ash out of the open window. Staring straight ahead, he exhaled. Despite the cold October air, a bead of sweat ran down behind his ear. "Just pay attention to what I fucking say," he said.

Red-beard's mirrored lenses stared back. He scratched his beard, and then nodded.

In his mind Raider-hat rehearsed details of the tunnel and the timing of the events that needed to happen over the next thirty minutes.

The tunnel is the only land access route for the town of Whittier. At two and a half miles, it is one of the longest tunnels in North America and dives deep under Maynard Mountain as a single rail line, built in the 1940s and later upgraded to allow vehicles. Car traffic travels out of Whittier on the top of the hour, and into Whittier on the half-hour.

After the last car exits the tunnel, it's closed for 15 minutes to allow turbo-jet-powered fans to suck the exhaust fumes out through ventilation shafts. Every 1600 ft there are safe houses in case of emergency, and traffic cameras monitor the tunnel constantly.

Raider-cap looked at Red-beard and asked him to repeat the timetable, the locations of the cameras, the sequence of markers, and the exact spot for the drop. He listened, tossed his cigarette out of the window, and lit up another. Satisfied with the recitation, he stared at the tunnel entrance in between glances at his watch. The car's AM/FM radio crackled out a country and western tune through tinny speakers, and Red-beard drummed his fingers on the steering wheel, almost in sync with the beat.

A bell rang and the gate ahead opened. One by one, the lanes of traffic filed into the tunnel. The Chevy idled, coughing out acrid, oily-blue smoke, awaiting its turn. Red-beard shifted the car into gear and the junker rumbled forward. The engine's fan belt squealed in protest as he turned the steering wheel and joined the end of the line of traffic entering the tunnel.

After they entered, Red-beard began counting out loud the section numbers on the walls of the tunnel. After four minutes, he said, "Next one, right?"

"Yes."

Red-beard nodded, and checked the rearview mirror. When they approached the marker, he slowed the car down to 5 mph, and looked over at Raider-cap – who pulled a floor-mounted handle, uncoupling the U-Haul from the trailer-hitch. The U-Haul screeched, flung up a few sparks, and ground to a halt in a blind spot between traffic cameras. Red-beard accelerated, rejoined the tail end of the traffic line, and five minutes later the Chevy exited the tunnel.

They both pulled their face coverings back up. As the gate came down, the turbo-fans inside the tunnel spooled up. They drove into Whittier and parked next to the marina.

Osler parked at the east end of the marina, and rose stiffly from the white Prius rental. He stretched his sore back and looked around. It was low tide and the odor of fish and kelp blew in with the cold air. Gulls wheeled and cried overhead. The gusty wind clacked and clanged halyards against the masts of sailboats moored in the marina, while frigid salt-water lapped at their hulls: familiar refrains of a seaside town.

One- and two-story wooden structures were clustered around the marina and either side of the railyard that split the town. Most were shut down for the winter season. All were somewhat worse for wear, with chipped and peeling paint, and warped boards. Plywood covered some of the windows.

Heavy clouds threatening snow hung low in the sky and obscured the tops of the mountains crowding the town against the horseshoe-shaped end of Passage Canal. The flat, dull light added to the cold, oppressive atmosphere. It was as if the collective forces of nature wanted to push the town out to sea and drown it.

Osler recalled a description of Whittier he had read when planning today's trip. In the 1940s, the sea connection to Prince William Sound, and the town's isolation, made Whittier an ideal location for a secret military base. The US Army bored a single rail tunnel through the mountains to a narrow strip of land next to the water, because the ice-free, deep-water harbor made an excellent all-season port. The base was self-sufficient, and the unrelenting bad weather prevented bombers – a big fear at the time – from finding the base. Over time, military capabilities changed, and the utility of Whittier vanished. So, in the 60s, when the military grew tired of it, they looked to turn it over to someone. Anyone. Please.

Visitors to Whittier tended to view the town in one of two ways: quaint or dismal. Osler favored the second. His eyes settled on a curiosity shop. A variety of signs, antlers, totems, and moose heads were stuck on the exterior like scrap metal on a junkyard electromagnet. It screamed *tourist trap*.

Osler walked up the steps, opened the door, and entered. At the sound of the door chimes, the proprietor, a weathered, wide-shouldered woman with a grey ponytail hanging halfway down her back, looked up from her phone. She finished the call, hung up, and welcomed Osler to the store.

The door chimes rang again, and an ancient man with a large twisted, walking stick entered, and limped and thumped over the uneven floorboards towards Ponytail. They struck up a conversation that had likely been played out thousands of times before. It was difficult to judge their ages. Osler guessed somewhere between 50 and 150 years old. The forces of nature up in Alaska were as brutal to skin as they were to buildings and granite.

Osler adjusted his wool cap, trying not to eavesdrop, and looked around the shop. Candles, seashells, candles-in-seashells, lumps of minerals, charms, native art, bracelets, books, maps, brochures, and dusty textiles populated the cramped space. A big glass display case stood at one end. From the low ceiling hung all manner of bags, towels, T-shirts, beads, and wind chimes.

A cloying musty odor of brine, mixed with lavender-scented candles, assailed his nostrils. Small windowpanes, clear in the center but dusty and smudged at the edges, revealed the choppy, white-capped harbor. Osler turned and banged his forehead into a set of wind chimes, then jumped back in alarm, knocking a bag to the floor.

"Sorry," he muttered, and picked it up as the furious cacophony of the disturbed wind chimes faded.

The woman laughed and said, "No problem. Can I help you find something?"

"Just browsing."

The old man and Ponytail went back to their discussion. Osler continued to poke around the shop. A display of mineral and gemstones caught his eye and he wandered over, careful not to trip on the uneven floor. He picked up a curious-looking stone and rolled it around in his palm. It had a squashed cubic shape, with sharp, even faces. Some of the faces were uniformly copper in color, and two were iridescent purple. The handwritten tag read: *Bornite (Peacock Ore) — the stone of happiness.*

"Oh, are you shittin' me? What a bunch of idiots!" said Ponytail.

"That's what the fella told me," said the old man.

Ponytail turned to Osler and said, "Sorry, didn't mean to be so loud. Walt was just giving me an update on the tunnel fire."

"Fire?" asked Osler.

"There's been a fire in the tunnel. Someone was hauling chemicals and their trailer-hitch broke. Dumb shits. Tunnel's shut down."

"How long until it opens?"

"Probably tomorrow."

"*What?* How do I get back to Anchorage?"

"You don't. Not tonight, anyway. Let me give Beatrice a call and see if she'll open up the inn for you. Most places have shut down for the winter, but I bet there's one or two other folks stuck here as well."

"Okay. Thanks," said Osler. He pulled out his smartphone and began texting his wife.

Ponytail picked up a corded phone and methodically poked at the handset. She listened, spoke for a bit and then hung up. "Left her a message," she said.

"I've got a flight out of Anchorage tomorrow. Is there a ferry or is it possible to charter a boat?" asked Osler.

"Nope. Ferry goes to Valdez, which won't help ya, and there's a big storm comin' tonight. No one's going out," answered Walt.

"Great."

The phone rang and Ponytail picked it up, nodded at Osler, and began chatting. Osler turned to his phone, which would only work on the roam setting here, and finished the text he'd been composing. *I'm going to be late. I need to reschedule my flight.* He hit the send button.

Why? R U hurt? came the reply.

Osler tapped his foot and pecked away at the screen, then hit send: *No. I already told you when I came off the mountain that I was fine. Nothing's changed.*

Then he felt a pang in his chest. *Her question was one of concern and love. She just wants me home safely, and so do I. I miss her. Why am I so irritable?*

Three reasons popped to mind immediately: one, he had not yet told his wife about his terrifying fall on the mountain, which – if not for the rope – would have left him permanently maimed or dead; two, he was trapped in a desolate town, when all he wanted was to get home, hug his wife and kiss her neck; and, three, he was obsessive about details and despised shortcuts – texts with letters subbing for words, such as *U* for *you,* always rubbed his fur the wrong way.

Sorry, I'm just upset about being stuck here. I love you and miss you, he texted.

Ok. Love U 2. Nice place?

Fishing village meets Siberian gulag, he typed.

Ponytail hung up the phone and said, "Beatrice said she'd open up the inn for you and the other folks that are stuck here. Good rate, too." She beckoned him over began sketching directions with a Sharpie on a glossy, three-fold tourist map, which Osler assumed could be found in every shop, store, and coffee shack in Whittier.

"Okay. Thanks," said Osler. "So, I'm stuck here, I guess. It's like the Covid-19 quarantine all over again."

"Huh?" said Walt.

"Covid-19; the quarantines and shutdowns? It only ended a few months ago," said Osler, wondering if there was a touch of senility at work here.

"Oh yeah. That's right. Ha ha," wheezed Walt. "Not much happened here. We're quarantined all the time anyway, ha ha. Isolated out here in the middle of nowhere."

"We call ourselves *Whidiots,* 'cause we're the only folks dumb enough to live here," laughed Ponytail. She beckoned Osler over and pointed through the grimy window. "See that building? All two hundred of us live there."

Osler looked at the multistory concrete structure, which resembled an asylum in a horror movie, and recalled the description of the Cold War remnant from a brochure. Begich

Towers, by far the largest structure in the town, had once been a fourteen-story barracks for the army. Now it housed the living quarters for the whole town, as well as the barber shop, grocery store, post office, mayor's office, the three-officer police station. It was as if a big, reinforced concrete bunker version of Noah's Ark had washed up on the shores from Prince William Sound during a storm.

"Looks pretty sturdy," was all Osler could think of to say.

"Yep. It's weathered a lot of storms," said Ponytail.

"Aye," added Walt. "It's a tough building. Even that earthquake in '64 couldn't bring it down, and it was too far uphill for those tsunami waves to reach. I was up there and saw all three waves come in and smash the town, one by one. First wave was the biggest. Hell, it was over forty feet high. Scared the bejesus out of me. Killed damn near a quarter of the town."

Osler continued to gaze out of the window. Dirty grey snow from a recent storm piled along the edges of the crushed gravel sidewalks and potholed streets, shoved there by plows and blowers. He remembered reading that 100 mph winds and many feet of snow sometimes came with the arctic storms that ripped into the tiny town.

A blast of wind hit the shop, rattling the antlers and other crap nailed to the outside and tinkling the windchimes suspended within. Ponytail looked up and said, "Weather's always shittier in Whittier."

She and Walt laughed.

Osler checked his watch: 5 pm. *It'll be dark in two hours.*

Osler thanked Ponytail for her help and left to find the inn. Outside, it was sleeting and blustery. He cinched up his Gore-Tex jacket and hood and walked to the rental car. He sat inside it for a few minutes while he consulted the map. Across the gravel lot, Ponytail was locking up the curiosity store.

Osler started the car and drove the length of the town along the marina, crossed over the railroad tracks, and drove the length of the town on the other side of the tracks to the inn. During the brief trip the car hadn't warmed up and he only made it halfway through *Four Horsemen* by the Clash. He pulled into the gravel lot, parked, and listened to the remaining one minute and thirty seconds of the song.

Inside the inn, the proprietor was helping a pair of cowboys, or, more accurately, a cowgirl and a cowboy. It seemed that these two were the only unlucky ones, besides Osler, to get trapped on the wrong side of the tunnel. They had gone all out on the Western-wear accoutrements: his and hers cowboy hats (black and white), blue denim jeans with ornate gold stitching, dinner-plate-sized silver belt buckles, checkered cotton shirts, and some expensive brand of cowboy boots. Wax-mustachioed Mr. Cowboy had on a long, black wool overcoat, which almost reached the floor, and a bolo tie.

Blonde Ms. Cowgirl wore a beige deer-suede fringe duster, and a pair of long-horn earrings.

Osler listened to Mr. Cowboy's nasal twang as he regaled the proprietor – who must be Beatrice – with stories of their Alaskan exploits to date. Ms. Cowgirl hiccupped and giggled, and then began adding in details that Mr. Cowboy had left out, like the shopping trips, and how they didn't have a such-and-such outlet store in Anchorage like they do all over Dallas.

Osler sighed. He suspected that the keyboard-punching, spreadsheet-wrangling, high-plains drifters were accountants, and the closest they had been to a real working ranch was watching Western drama mini-series on cable.

The wind howled outside, and sleet pattered the windows.

Beatrice cautioned them about the storm. Cowgirl gave her a vacant stare for a few seconds, likely indicating that extensive inter-neuron communications were occurring and that a thought was forthcoming. She turned to Cowboy. "Hey honey, let's have a hurricane party!" she said.

Cowboy responded with a whoop, and slapped Cowgirl on the ass. They both laughed. Cowboy spelled out the list of ingredients they would need. Beatrice pointed them over to the Towers and told them about the grocery store inside. Cowboy asked about a specific tequila brand. Beatrice shrugged. Osler wished they would just get out of the way.

Finally, the two cowpokes finished yakking and moved away from the counter. Cowboy turned to Osler and said, "Hey. You wanna join the party? What's your name, fella?"

"Osler. Alfred Osler," said Osler, sticking out his hand.

Cowboy jumped back six feet, like he'd been bitten by a rattlesnake.

Osler saw his mistake and apologized. Distracted by the circumstances he had forgotten that times, culture, and humanity had forever changed. In his practice as neurologist he was meticulous in hand washing and taking every sensible precaution. But he was on vacation and away from his clinical routine. His mind was still in Denali National Park, where he'd spent the last week hiking and climbing with a guided mountaineering group. 'Social distancing' was a phrase he'd forgotten in the cramped tents and glacier travel with his 'fellowship of the rope' teammates.

It occurred to him that handshakes had transformed into the equivalent of the middle-finger. A handshake used to mean *I am unarmed*, and had been a symbol of trust. Now it meant an offer of transmissible plague: *Want to shake hands and die?*

The upside of Osler's public health faux-pas was that now he wasn't likely to get slapped on the bottom, thumped between the shoulder blades, or whatever else passed for pleasantries in Dallas-land.

Recovered from his scare, Cowboy laughed and finished the invitation by giving Osler their room number and telling him to stop by later. Then the white-hat and black-hat outlaw gang tickled and laughed their way out of the inn in search of margarita ingredients. Osler hadn't the heart to tell Cowgirl that the storm wasn't actually a tropical hurricane. *Why spoil the party?*

Beatrice shook her head, and chuckled. "Kids."

Osler considered this but said nothing about the cowpoke-actuaries. He signed the hotel policy checklist and waiver, and paid. Beatrice got him his key. The wind gusted and the whole inn vibrated with the force. A storm shutter banged a few times. He thanked her for opening up the inn, and she waved him off, stating that she was happy to help.

"We close the hotel for guests in October, but the restaurant stays open all year for the locals," she said. "The fish and chips are excellent."

Osler thanked her and carried his luggage upstairs. The floorboards creaked as he opened the door and entered his room. The building groaned under another blast. He decided he was hungry and went down to the restaurant.

Raider-cap adjusted his heavy backpack and handed Red-beard a 12-pack of Alaskan Brewing Co. Kölsch as they approached the cash register.

A man and a woman in cowboy hats entered the store and stopped to look around. Raider-cap glanced over. *Get a load of these two idiots.* He nudged Red-beard, tilted his head in their direction, and smirked.

Cowboy looked around the store, whistled and said, "Slim pickings."

"It'll be fine, honey," giggled Cowgirl, and went to the liquor aisle.

Cowboy turned around and his eyes locked on Raider-cap, then his gaze flicked up to the black hat. He chuckled and said, "Whoo-whee, the Cowboys are gonna kick your ass this year, 'cause y'all are playing us in Texas Stadium. Cowboys always get their outlaws."

Raider-cap stared at him, ground his teeth. *If it wouldn't ruin the gig, I would fuckin' gut you like a pig.* Cowboy grinned back, and opened his mouth but was interrupted by a call from Cowgirl: "Hey honey, Don Julio or Jose Cuervo?"

"I'm comin', baby," he said and went over to join her.

Raider-cap stared for a few more seconds, then turned and walked wordlessly toward the cash register. Red-beard plopped down the 12-pack and the clerk rang up the purchase.

"Where're you guys staying?" asked the clerk.

"Why?" asked Raider-cap, tossing a twenty-dollar bill onto the counter.

"Well. It's just that you're not from here, tunnel's down, and there's a storm coming. Didn't mean nothin' by it," answered the clerk. He finished the transaction and passed the change back in a gloved hand.

"We're staying on a boat in the marina."

"Well, good luck then. I wouldn't want to be on a boat tonight," said the clerk. "Be safe."

"We plan on it."

Raider-cap glanced over his shoulder as they left the grocery store. In the hallway, he looked in both directions and then ushered Red-beard towards a metal door. Once through, they began descending the concrete stairwell. "IT closet's in the basement," said Raider-cap, and produced a key from his pocket. "I want things set up within an hour. Got it?"

"I hear you."

Osler opened the door and stepped into the dimly-lit restaurant. The layout and motif were decidedly 1970s. Along one wall was a long, horizontal slot which offered a narrow glimpse into the kitchen where a fat man in a greasy white apron alternated his attention between burners, fryers, and the sitcom playing on a small TV. Along another wall of the restaurant was a counter and the cash register. Conversation had stopped by the time Osler had stepped fully inside.

The waitress told him that he could sit anywhere. Every other table was blocked off with yellow caution tape to enforce social distancing. Only about half of the remaining non-quarantine, red-vinyl-covered tables were occupied by patrons. Osler moved to a table in the corner, noting that conversation had not yet resumed. He sat down and studied the menu.

Something hovered next to him, blocking the light. An ancient woman sat down across from Osler. She put a deck of Tarot cards on the table.

Osler raised his eyebrows and said, "Hello."

She squinted, turned her head to fix her rheumy left eye on him, and said, "Shh. Listen."

From the top of the deck, she laid out cards. First, she plunked down the Fool, and next, the Tower. She tapped each with a thunk of her gnarled right index finger. She turned over one more card, Justice, and gasped. "He is coming tonight. The captain," she said.

Osler wasn't sure how to react. The woman stared at him, then gathered her cards, stood and left. Muted conversations and the clinking of dinnerware resumed.

"Sorry about that," said the waitress, who suddenly appeared at Osler's elbow. She splashed water into his plastic tumbler from a pitcher, getting most of it in the cup. "She's been here about two weeks. Telling fortunes and spinning her tales."

"Oh?" asked Osler. "What tales?"

"Stories about the SS *Baychimo*. She keeps saying the captain is coming on October 31st. It's got the whole town freaked out. We're not over all that mess from Covid yet, and folks here are mistrustful of strangers. No offense. Anyway, she shows up and starts telling us all about that damned ghost ship. And now there's a storm coming, which she says confirms the prophecy. Hell, it storms all the damned time up here, 'cept for July. Some fortune teller, huh?"

Osler nodded politely and looked at his menu.

"What would you like?"

"Fish and chips, please," he said.

"Good choice. It's my favorite here," said the waitress. She gathered up his menu and left. Osler looked around the room and tried to imagine what it must be like to live and work in Whittier. As he attempted to shut out all the voices and noise in the room, his phone vibrated. He tapped out a reply to his wife, still bubbling about the climbing he'd experienced and trying to describe all the details — minus the mishap, of course — within the limited format of text messages.

It was frustrating, and he paused. He enjoyed telling rich stories, using hand gestures to illustrate important points. His wife told him how cute he was when he was in full, animated mode; eyebrows dancing up and down, and arms waving like an orchestra conductor. Osler smiled at the memory.

He turned back to the phone and busily tapped out a short essay on what it had felt like to land on the Talkeetna Glacier in a Cessna equipped with skis. Reliving the experience gave him goose bumps. He typed more, hitting the send button whenever the screen balked at accepting any further characters.

The waitress came back with his fish and chips. Osler inhaled the aroma from the golden batter-crusted cod and sprinkled on some malt vinegar. He munched his meal in between exchanging texts with his wife. He was trying to not listen to the conversations around him, but the effort was proving difficult. He sighed.

Osler possessed excellent hearing, but his remarkable abilities went far beyond that. The processing centers in the auditory cortex of his brain were able to identify, organize, and categorize sounds to the point he could follow ten different individual conversations in a crowded, noisy room. This had helped him in many ways but had almost driven him mad on several occasions.

He finished his meal and looked up to see Beatrice come down the stairs and approach a young woman working the cash register. He watched the two women converse in American Sign Language. He noted the similarities in their body morphology and concluded they were likely genetically related, probably mother and daughter.

The waitress came over with the check and directed him to pay at the till. Osler thanked her and approached the cash register. The young woman looked up with a surly expression. As he got closer, he noted that she had one blue eye and one brown one, and a white streak in the middle of her otherwise brunette hair. *Waardenburg syndrome*, he thought.

She stared at him. He imagined her expression was a defensive warning. *She's probably tired of strangers reacting to her unique appearance. She's probably been teased and ridiculed her whole life.*

She held her hand out for the check. Osler signed to her that he had enjoyed the meal and was grateful be able to stay at the Inn tonight.

"You're welcome," she signed back.

She rang up the check, showed him the amount, then signed, "How do you know ASL?"

"I'm a neurologist, studying hearing centers in the brain," he signed.

"Interesting!"

"Yes. I love my work!"

She smiled and asked him his name.

"Alfred. Yours?"

"Kalliope," she signed.

"A beautiful name."

Kalliope shrugged. Osler handed her his credit card and indicated that he wanted to include a tip. He hoped he hadn't embarrassed her. She handed him the receipt and he added his signature. Kalliope signed, "I'm studying biology in college. I want to be a doctor."

Osler smiled and signed, "What school?"

"University of Michigan. I came home because…"

"Virus? Still no classes," he signed, interrupting her.

She scowled and nodded. Kalliope told him about her school and that she loved biology. Osler told her about his work at the Texas Medical Center in Houston. Their conversation was interrupted by a couple who needed to pay. Osler stepped aside.

After the couple left, Kalliope and Osler resumed their chat. She offered him a chair and he sat down. Osler learned that Beatrice was indeed Kalliope's mother, and that the economic collapse had hit the town hard. Summer tourism had been a boon, but no longer. There used to be full tours, cruise ships, and ferries. People came to see the natural splendor of mountains, hanging glaciers, Prince William Sound, and orcas. But no more. Everything had changed.

"Why do you want to be a doctor?" signed Osler.

"I want to help people like me."

Osler smiled, and signed, "That's a great reason to be a physician."

Another group came up to pay. Osler thanked Kalliope for the chat and bid her goodnight.

Kalliope signed, "People can get a little crazy here. Goodnight. Be safe."

Osler left the restaurant and walked up the stairs to his room. He stopped at the door of the urban cowboys and knocked, but got no reply. He went to his room and keyed himself in. Wind vibrated the inn and hail clacked against the windows. Osler prepared for bed.

He pulled back the covers and lay down. He turned off the bedside lamp and tried to ignore all the sounds in the inn. But he couldn't. Every groan, creak, or footstep on a stair penetrated his thoughts. Even the faint conversation in the lobby tickled his brain. He sighed and reached for his high-end, noise-cancelling headphones. *I don't know how I managed before these were invented.*

At 4 am, a chirping sound penetrated Osler's dreams. He sat up in bed and was confused until he realized that it was coming from his headphones. He'd forgotten to turn this smartphone alarm off, and it was dutifully Wi-Fi broadcasting to the headphones. He thumbed off the alarm and got up to look out of the window. The storm had waned, and beneath the streetlamp he could see only a light flurry falling, but there was a good two feet of fresh snow on the ground.

He removed his headphones and heard a keening wail. The noise of the wind from the storm had abated and in its place was a repetitive, wailing sound. As he listened to the noise, and tried to identify it, he found it soothing. There was something oddly peaceful in the notes. He yawned and sat back down on the bed. Out of habit he slipped the headphones back over his ears as he lay down. But then the desire to close his eyes and sleep dissolved.

Osler lay in bed, wide awake, and puzzled over the mystery. His brain ran through the sounds, replayed them, and his acoustic processors analyzed the patterns. He frowned.

And then he raised his eyebrows.

The sound was from a colleague's research in the field, but he'd never heard of anything actually strong enough to do what he'd just experienced. *Someone is broadcasting a frequency to induce theta brainwaves, for hypnosis. But who would use these sonic techniques here? And why?*

He dressed and grabbed his parka. Still wearing his headphones, he walked down to the lobby and found it empty. He pulled the headphones from his ears and confirmed that the sound was still there. Something moved in his peripheral vision and he turned to see Kalliope storm up the stairs from the restaurant, dressed in full winter clothes. She turned to face him. She looked upset.

He signed, "Hello. What's wrong?"

She signed that she got up early to check on the inn, and saw a stranger outside with a rifle. She went to the police station, but it was closed. She went to her mother but was unable to wake her.

"You're a doctor. She needs help," she signed.

He asked her to lead the way to the Towers. Outside the inn, he slid the headphones from his ears briefly, and found the sound was louder than inside the inn. Plunging through the fresh snow, Kalliope led them along a path. As they turned a corner, Kalliope pushed him back into the darkness, away from the glare of a streetlight. She put a finger to her lips and pointed to two men with rifles, who were walking away from them towards the marina. As the men moved under a streetlight, Osler saw they wore bulky black clothing with large hoods.

After the men had disappeared, Osler and Kalliope resumed their trek to the Towers. Inside, Osler confirmed that the sound was present here as well. Exploring further, he noted a speaker in the ceiling. Shifting a plastic milk crate and standing on it to rest his fingers against the speaker, the vibrations told him that the internal public-address system was the source of the sound inside the building. *Strange. And what's the source outside?*

They checked on Beatrice, and Osler found her as Kalliope had described: somnolent. She mumbled when Osler pinched her skin but wouldn't wake up. Her pulse and breathing were normal, but he couldn't rouse her. Osler signed to Kalliope about the speakers and the sound that was keeping everyone asleep.

"Not possible," she signed back.

"Yes," he signed. "Trust me. Please take me to the police office."

Kalliope led him out of her mother's apartment and down the hallway. The office was on the first floor and they took the stairs down.

They found the office locked. Osler looked through the transparent plexiglass window and couldn't see anyone inside. Kalliope banged on the door and moved around to look through the window from different angles. Osler thought, *This is a mass hypnosis event – and the town was already primed by the viral pandemic and then the fortune teller. But who has this level of technology? And why here?*

"The police might be patrolling outside," signed Kalliope.

"OK. Let's check."

Outside, they found the light snow had stopped and a crystalline ice fog hung in the frigid air: visibility was poor. Osler knew they needed to be cautious about blundering into the men with the rifles, so he signed to Kalliope about being alert. She nodded. Osler felt vulnerable without his sensitive hearing, but he couldn't risk taking the headphones off. He would have to rely on his other senses. They moved slowly towards the marina and encountered two pairs of deep boot imprints that went along Depot Road towards the commercial dock near the end of the railyard.

Kalliope led Osler away from the boot tracks, into the pedestrian tunnel underneath the railyard. The corrugated cylindrical passage, lit by a row of bright lights hanging from the center, had a decidedly Cold War feel. At the other end, they emerged onto a snow-covered ramp that led up to a large parking lot.

Moving lights to the right attracted Osler's attention. He crouched down next to Kalliope, who had already hidden herself behind a low wall, and watched a forklift carrying a large box back away from a railcar and then turn to head towards a ship at the commercial dock. Two men with rifles paced along next to the forklift, and a third climbed into the opening in the freight car and disappeared.

On the railcar was a yellow diamond, in the center of which was a black circle with three black blades, like a fan: the trefoil symbol of the international warning sign for radioactivity. Osler looked at Kalliope, whose eyes had widened.

They watched until the forklift was a safe distance away, then ascended the rest of the ramp. The snow thinned to ankle deep as they stepped out onto the parking lot. The winds had swept most of the snow into rounded drifts at the west end of the lot.

Kalliope beckoned for him to follow and snuck across the lot in a crouch. Osler paused. He thought about the wisdom of creeping around in the dark, early morning hours with a young deaf woman – trying to find the sole police officer on duty in an isolated, frozen Alaskan town – while men with firearms were stealing radioactive cargo from a train. Not to mention that the technology to accomplish hypnosis with sound – something that had previously only been theoretical to Osler – meant that this had to be a very high-stakes crime.

He knelt down in the snow.

This is too dangerous. I'll catch up with Kalliope and tell her we should hide until this is over.

Then: *That's fear speaking: you're still scared by the crevasse fall.*

The memory flooded his mind, of the snow suddenly collapsing underneath him, plunging him into a gaping maw in the ice until the rope attached to his teammates jerked taut, slamming him into the crevasse wall like a pendulum. If they hadn't arrested his fall, he and the entire rope team would have plunged to their deaths.

You can't abandon this.

Not my duty.

Yes, it is.

Osler exhaled a deep breath that he hadn't realized he'd been holding, and rose to follow Kalliope's tracks. When he reached her, she tugged on the sleeve of his parka and pointed excitedly ahead – and then slunk off again. He looked and saw two faint red lights that looked, from here, like distant embers in the darkness.

When he caught up with her again, they were only a stone's throw from a black and white SUV: the police vehicle. Kalliope looked back to the railyard, then tapped Osler's shoulder and pointed out the two men they had seen earlier with the rifles; they were moving back towards the Towers.

Kalliope and Osler crouched lower. The men had flashlights and were returning along the exact same pathway they had taken earlier: Depot Road. Osler looked at Kalliope, who pointed to her boots, and he nodded his understanding. The men would soon find their boot tracks on the other side of the pedestrian tunnel, and be alerted to their presence. Osler estimated that they would need to cover only a hundred yards before the discovery.

Kalliope rapidly signed a plan. Osler thought for a moment and then gave a thumbs-up. *This just keeps getting deeper. I should have backed out when I had the chance.*

He crouched and shuffled towards the police cruiser, and opened the driver's door carefully, to find a sleeping policewoman. His eyes went to her belt: holstered on her left hip was the largest handgun he'd ever seen. *I need keys, not guns*, he thought. He peered at the opposite hip, and was rewarded by the glint of a large silver ring. He unclipped the carabiner attachment and lifted ten pounds of tethered brass keys.

Slinking back towards Kalliope, he stopped, and almost tore a rotator cuff tossing her the keys.

"Good luck," he signed.

She nodded. "You too."

Osler moved back to the idling police vehicle, knelt by the open door and looked back to watch Kalliope move west. She picked her way across the rail tracks and disappeared behind the engine, out of sight from the unloading operation at the opposite end. Osler turned to the policewoman and unbuckled her seatbelt. He pulled her out of the vehicle. Grunting with effort, he dragged her through the snow towards two parked vehicles.

He looked up to see the beams of two flashlights sweep rapidly back and forth over the snow, on the other side of the train tracks, near the Towers. He took off his parka, tucked it around the policewoman like a blanket, and moved back to the SUV.

Inside, he ran his fingers over the control panel.

Lights. Lights. Where are the fucking lights?

Part one complete, thought Kalliope. She looked at the keys crowding the ring in her hand. *Now for outside help. Osler and I can't do this on our own.*

She crept back through the snow towards the Towers. Every ten paces or so she stopped and looked towards the dock. Near the Towers, she halted and peered towards where she had left Osler; across the railyard and on the far side of the snowy parking lot; a half-mile away. The fog had cleared a bit and she thought she could perhaps see the faint taillights of the SUV.

She flinched as two men with rifles slung on their shoulders popped into view under the light of the south side of the pedestrian tunnel, scarcely a hundred yards away. They stopped. One gesticulated at the other, and then shoved him backwards. They grabbed each other and fought.

Blue and red strobe lights pierced the darkness, attracting Kalliope's gaze to the police SUV. She smiled. *That'll get their attention. But Osler's got to hurry.*

Raider-cap stopped in his tracks as he came across two pairs of fresh footprints leading to the pedestrian tunnel.

What the fuck.

He thumped Red-beard on the shoulder, gestured at the tracks, and pointed a finger at his headphones. Both he and Red-beard removed them just long enough for Raider-cap to

154

say, "People are up. This sound shit ain't working. Time to kill."

Red-beard shook his head.

Raider-cap shoved him against a wall. Red-beard pushed off the wall and bounded back. They grappled; each trying to throw the other to the ground as if it were some kind of frozen-tundra judo match.

And then Raider-cap stopped and stared at the red and blue flashing lights across the railyard, in the parking lot. Wrestling forgotten for the moment, he pointed at his ear again, and they both removed their headphones.

"Pigs die first," said Raider-cap. "Get back to the ship and get 'er ready to sail. We gotta move!"

Raider-cap cycled the action on the Kalashnikov assault-rifle – chambering a round – thumbed off the safety to full-auto, and moved into the tunnel.

Osler sat in the driver's seat of the vehicle, closed the door, and fastened the seatbelt. Staccato blue and red flashes reflected off the snow. He paused, held his breath and looked out the back window and then the side mirrors for signs of the men he was certain were coming. Urgency tightened his throat. *I need to drive to the far western edge of the lot, park, and get the hell away.*

He put his foot on the brake, grasped the gearstick, shifted into drive, and eased off the brake. The SUV rolled forward.

The passenger-side window suddenly disappeared, and Osler flinched as a pressure wave slapped his face. A swath of the right side of windshield crazed white as opaque spider webs burst around finger-sized holes. Pain lanced through his right thigh and something was burning his neck.

Osler glanced over and saw that the passenger-side half of the dashboard looked like it had suffered a shark attack – and glass fragments were scattered everywhere.

Crap – they're shooting at me.

Osler punched the accelerator and the SUV shot forward. He was pushed back in his seat, and then slung sideways. A disorienting rotation brought nauseating panic. The headlights of the SUV illuminated a series of images: a snow-covered car, a boarded-up building, a rusted-out sailboat, and a man with a gun flashing small sunbursts at him.

Kalliope made it the rest of the way to the Towers and then turned to check Osler's progress. She was startled to see the SUV moving across the lot, out of control, spinning like a top. *Maybe he doesn't know how to drive on snow and ice,* she thought. *Come on, get it under control.*

Her heart pounded in her chest.

Strobic yellow flashes jumped out from a man pointing a rifle at the spinning police-SUV.

My God!

She opened her mouth and screamed a wordless wail of fear and fled into the Towers.

Osler felt like his stomach was storming north to invade his chest cavity, and then he felt himself thrown sideways. His head smashed against the driver's-side window as the SUV careened off a parked car, and a high-pitched ringing sound assaulted his ears.

The nauseating spin slowed, and Osler saw buildings flip by as the vehicle continued to slide along the parking lot. He felt detached, as if he was watching himself from a distance.

He got a second glimpse of the gunman as the SUV completed another rotation, but thankfully he was now much further away. Osler's disorientation faded and he steered into the direction of the spin with white knuckles. The SUV fishtailed back and forth a few times before yielding control back to the driver. With the vehicle finally straightened up, and the distance from the gunman increasing, Osler looked up in horror to see large white mounds approaching at high speed.

He panic-stomped the brakes, which did nothing to change the velocity, and the SUV plowed into a large snowdrift, at which point he was punched in the face by a big white boxing glove.

Stunned, he tried to figure out what was going on.

White powder hung in the air and dusted the cabin. Osler felt like molasses in winter. He flung the door open, pushed past the collapsed airbag, and tumbled out into the snow.

The ringing in his ears faded and then everything became loud. The police siren screamed at him as he rose to a low crouch beside his crushed headphones.

He peered cautiously around the back of the vehicle and saw the gunman, a hundred yards away, running at full tilt towards him. Osler shifted his weight and collapsed. His right thigh seared with pain, and he reached down to feel warm wetness on his jeans. *I've been shot!*

He crept on all fours and peered around the bumper in time to see his assailant slip and flop onto the snow.

Now's my chance. Osler steeled himself and rose, grunting in pain. He turned and lurched toward a low part of a snowdrift, aiming for the row of buildings just beyond it.

As he got closer, he spied an alley between two of the buildings and headed towards it. His ears registered the abrupt *pop-pop* of gunfire layered on top of the deafening *woo-woo* of the police siren, which he must have triggered in his frenetic search to activate the lights. And in the split second between the siren tones was the faint wail of the hypnosis waveform.

Osler limped into the alley and stopped to brace his back against the wall. He took off his gloves and then glanced back around the corner. His assailant had stopped firing and was stalking, weapon raised, towards the SUV. Osler explored his thigh with his fingertips and found two holes in his flesh. *Entry and exit wound.*

He cursed at the pain and glanced back again. The gunman was almost at the SUV. Osler also noted that his own tracks through the snow would lead the gunman straight to him. He retreated further into the alleyway. *I have to keep going, but I can't outrun him.*

Then the police siren stopped. Osler swore and limped along. *He's at the police car and he'll come here next.* Blood dripped from his thigh.

He felt dizzy, and staggered.

The lullaby waveform began to worm into his ears; caressing his brain; soothing the pain. Osler struggled forward against the sound.

No. I can't fall asleep: I'll die.

He took ten more unsteady steps and stumbled around the corner of a building – and fell sideways into a snow drift. His eyes closed.

So tired. I feel warm. Comfortable…

Odysseus asked his men to plug their ears with beeswax and lash him to the main mast. The men understood and obeyed his command: No matter how much I beg or threaten, do not release me, for the sirens' song is death.

Kalliope ran to the police office, threw off her gloves, and with shaking hands, extracted the heavy key ring. *Why can't cops just have a few keys and not a thousand?*

She tried one key; then another; then another. She cycled to the next one, and her breath caught as it went halfway into the lock – and then stopped. She pushed harder, to no avail. *Damn it!*

She tried to pull it out, but it was stuck. Moaning in frustration, she kicked the door and grabbed the key with both hands. Leaning back, she yanked hard. Pain stabbed into her left index finger, and she nearly toppled backwards as the key popped out.

Kalliope felt wetness on her left hand and raised it to see blood. She put the injured finger in her mouth. Her taste buds registered metallic sweetness and probing with the tip of her tongue told her that the wound was small, and shallow.

Withdrawing the finger, she went back to the task at hand and looked for a similar match to the key that had almost worked. Red dripped from her finger onto the carpeted floor.

Here. This one.

Small vibrations tickled her fingers as the key sank into the cylinder. She twisted it and the door opened. *Yes!*

Inside, she flipped the light switch, and fluorescent bulbs flickered to life. Grabbing a few tissues from a box to wrap around her finger, she looked over the objects in the office: a large L-shaped desk supporting two big, flat-panel monitors;

an array of black boxes mounted on a rack, with glowing LEDs; and CCTV screens in a 4 x 4 rectangular grid showing three black and white feeds – the other thirteen screens were black. The grainy feeds showed the Whittier-side tunnel entrance, the west end of the marina, and the front of the Towers – but no people.

One of the flat-panel monitors displayed a teal torus that spun slowly and bounced across the black screen. She moved closer and saw that the 3D shape had red, white, and blue dots on one side. She snickered when she realized it was a doughnut.

Kalliope sat down and grabbed the mouse; the screensaver disappeared and was replaced by a rectangular text box and a password prompt. On a whim, she typed, *doughnut*. The box wiggled from side to side, like a person shaking their head. Undeterred, she tried a few different spellings of doughnut, but got the same result. She bit the corner of her lip, and tried *password*, *admin*, and *WPD*. No luck.

She slung the keyboard away, banged the mouse down, and stood. *Come on – there has to be some way to summon help.* Her eyes drifted to the array of black metal boxes. One had a cable leading to a large silver microphone on a black stand, perched on the desk. *Not helpful.* Then a blue and white icon on one of the boxes caught her attention. It depicted a stick figure running up a hill, being pursued by three small waves, and one very large one: a tsunami warning sign. She rushed over to inspect the console further.

The tsunami warning system is automatically triggered by an earthquake, but they test the system once a month – and then everyone bitches about it on Facebook. Maybe I can set it off.

Her breathing quickened.

A squat, silver cylindrical key stuck out from a circular plate, the size of a quarter, on the face of the unit. She read the labels: currently it was set to *Auto*. She rotated the key clockwise until a white arrow moved 90 degrees to point at a mark labelled *Activate*, then pressed an adjacent red, backlit button labelled *Alert*. The button pulsed red, and bright white strobes began flashing in the office and out in the hallway.

Excellent!

Kalliope turned around and was surprised to see that lights on the phone were flashing and several windows on the computer workstation had popped open. Text scrolled on one of them, and she sat down to read it: *<USCG Valdez Dispatch> We're picking up a tsunami alert from your station. Please respond.*

She sat down and began typing a reply to the Coast Guard.

Horns blew. And echoed.

Horns blew and the walls of Jericho shook.

Horns blew and the priests chanted. Dust shook loose from the walls...

A klaxon blared.

Osler opened his eyes.

He sat upright and winced in pain. The klaxon sounded again, and after a heartbeat of silence, echoes rumbled off of the tall ring of mountains. He looked at his injured leg, which was still dripping blood, and saw a fist-sized crimson hole in the snow underneath.

How much blood have I lost? What is that horn? Why...?

The klaxon sounded again. Osler thought of the tale Walt had told about the '64 tsunami. He rolled to his knees and slowly got to his feet. He shook his head and braced against a wall as a wave of fatigue threatened to send him to the ground again; after it passed, he took a few tentative steps. He limped around the corner of the building and looked back down the alley, expecting to see his assailant – or perhaps to get hypnotized again – at any second.

Maybe the tsunami warning is drowning out the hypnosis wave; and the police siren did the same thing.

He waited, panting in pain, as the klaxons blared. He counted out thirty seconds. *I'm still awake. But if there's a tsunami on the way, I'm hosed.*

Osler stumbled back towards the police SUV. When he emerged from the alley, he caught a brief glimpse of a man under a distant streetlight, running east.

❖

Raider-cap boarded the trawler, slammed his headphones on the deck, and accosted the first crew member he encountered.

"Hurry the fuck up. Let's go!" he yelled, and stormed towards the bridge. He took three paces, stopped and looked at a large array of PA speakers mounted on the deck. He ejected a magazine from his assault rifle and inserted a fresh one. Crew scattered.

Raider-cap screamed as he opened fire. The speakers erupted in sparks and splinters. He continued to hold down the trigger until the magazine was empty, and then he continued towards the bridge. *Why am I always surrounded by fucking idiots?*

Klaxons blared and echoed. Raider-cap opened the hatch to the bridge and entered. The captain was sitting in a chair anchored to the deck, and he was hunched over the main console. A crooked headset covered only one of his ears, and he was studying a screen. Fat rolls on his neck shifted as he turned to look over his shoulder with a scowling, deeply-lined face and said, "Nothing on NOAA. No earthquake. Must be a false alarm." He turned his attention back to the console.

"Fuckin' cop must've done it," said Raider-cap, and spat on the deck. "I lit him up. Hope he bleeds to death." He looked out at Whittier through a porthole, paced around the small bridge, then settled in front of the navigation console. He pressed buttons on the radar unit, and the captain's patience.

"Can you check that the cargo's secure?" asked the captain. "Wit' all your shooting, you might've damaged your precious stuff."

"Don't order me around, old man."

"The safety of this vessel and crew are my responsibility. I don't need no hot head jeopardizing—"

The captain was cut off by the muzzle of a 45-caliber semi-automatic pistol pushed into his throat, under the angle of his jaw.

"I'm in charge," hissed Raider-cap. "You know who you're fucking working for, right? Never forget you are expendable!"

Raider-cap pulled the gun away.

The captain rose from his chair to stand at full height. Raider-cap hammered the captain's temple with the butt of the pistol. The captain staggered under the blow and gripped the console's edge. Blood seeped down the side of his face and dripped onto his wool sweater. He turned to stare at Raider-cap, and said, "Get off my bridge."

Raider-cap sneered. "I'm checking below. Make this bucket of trash move!"

He exited the bridge into a frigid, salty wind, and halted next to the starboard railing. A popping noise attracted his attention and he looked aft at the snapping Jolly-Roger on the poop deck. He paused to admire the middle finger iconography that had been overlaid on the traditional pirate theme. It spoke to him.

Raider-cap turned to gaze above the bow. On the horizon, the pre-dawn glow painted the retreating storm clouds pink; straight ahead was a fog bank. *We won't be found in there. Let's hope the captain knows the waters here as well as he claims.*

The dock receded as the trawler pulled away. The frequency of vibrations throughout the ship quickened as the engines churned out more horsepower and the vessel buffeted through the choppy waters. He gripped the rigging and thought, *Finally, the moment is here. The plundering capitalists will shit themselves when we unleash our wrath.*

Osler limped back through the snow drift. He trembled in response to the cold, the pain, and the adrenaline being dumped into his veins – and due to his worries about the severity of the gunshot, and whether he was about to be flattened by a massive wall of water. The acoustic processors in his brain noted the absence of the hypnosis wave, in the small space of silence in between the blasts of the klaxons, but he was too occupied with survival to give it much thought.

His eyes flicked up and he paused briefly to watch the ship pull away from the dock. He pivoted and was startled to see a policewoman stomping across the parking lot toward him, with an angry face and a drawn gun.

"Freeze!" she ordered.

Shaking and teeth chattering, he raised his arms. "I'm... not armed."

"Then who the hell shot up my vehicle?" demanded the officer.

"The men... on the... ship," Osler stuttered, and slowly tilted his head to the left, in the direction of the departing ship. He gasped in a breath.

"What?"

"The men on that boat... stole something radioactive... from the train... shot up your SUV... and shot me," he panted. "I'm a doctor. I'm trying to help... I've been working with Kalliope..."

"Kalliope?"

Osler nodded. The radio attached to the officer's shoulder suddenly squawked. She pressed a button on the unit and flexed her neck so that her chin was almost on her shoulder, and said, "Sergeant Mallory, Whittier PD."

She backed away from Osler to continue the conversation; her eyes never left him, and the pistol stayed pointed in his direction. She nodded a few times. Osler's mouth felt like cotton. He trembled and then another wave of lightheadedness hit him, and the periphery of his vision greyed. *If I don't sit, I'm going to pass out.*

He studied the officer for signs of objection as he slowly sat down and hugged his knees. *Am I going to bleed to death or drown in a tsunami?*

Sgt. Mallory straightened her neck, lowered her weapon, and re-holstered it. She approached Osler, studying him with her brown eyes.

"That was the Coast Guard," she said. "Kalliope's the one that set off the alert; there's no tsunami danger."

Osler mumbled, "That's great."

"You're hurt. Let's get you over to my vehicle."

He smiled weakly and accepted the offered hand. He groaned and stood. Sgt. Mallory put her arm around him, and he hugged her for support. Although he was taller and heavier than the officer, he felt the strength in her stance. They shuffled, as if performing a slow dance, towards the damaged black and white police SUV. Osler carefully studied the placement of his feet on the ground to make sure he stayed upright. As they approached the passenger side of the SUV, he looked up and saw the effects of the violence from a different perspective: the tires were flat, all the windows were shot out, the metalwork resembled the surface of a large colander, and the engine hissed steam.

Shit!

"It's Osler, isn't it?" she asked. "Your name?"

"Yes." He stumbled.

She propped him against the vehicle. "Osler, let's get you in the backseat, and I'll get the first aid kit." She opened the rear door, studied his face briefly, and then swept glass out of the way.

He felt her arms easing him onto the seat and then into a horizontal position. The fog around his brain began to lift, each heartbeat bringing a little more blood flow.

"I need to hear about what you saw, especially the stolen cargo and the ship," she said,

"Ok," he said. "I'm a doctor … can you hand me the first aid kit?"

Osler nodded his thanks as she gave him the kit. His breathing became easier and he propped himself up against the opposite door; he opened the kit and extracted a pair of bandage scissors, several packages of gauze, and a roll of two-inch paper tape.

Sgt. Mallory watched him as he set about cutting through his jeans to expose the wounds. He winced as he pressed small gauze pads over the wounds.

"Last thing I remember is a trawler, a big one, maybe ninety foot or more, pulling in. I don't see it now," she said. "Was that the ship?"

Osler didn't know what a trawler was, and his expression must have demonstrated it.

"Big mast, and two booms, amidships, forming a *V*," she said.

Osler nodded.

"Okay. Tell me about the cargo."

"I couldn't see the cargo on the forklift, but the train car had a radiation symbol." He was a little giddy and distracted by the work of bandaging – and the pain – and sensed he was babbling. His hands shook as he added two big wads of folded gauze 4x4s to the two wounds, and began circling the tape around and around his thigh to finish securing the pressure dressing.

Sgt. Mallory nodded. "The Coast Guard said something about a sound that made us all fall asleep; got that from Kalliope. Of course, she can't hear, so I reckon she got that idea from you."

"It's a hypnosis wave form that induces theta waves in our brains and functions as a soporific," he replied, then noted the officer's blank face. "Kind of like a sleeping pill."

"Hmm," she said, frowning. "You okay? You look pale."

"I think I need to go to the hospital."

"Yes, I think you do, too," she said, and reached for the communication console in the SUV. "Coast Guard Valdez, this is Sgt. Mallory. Over."

The SUV speakers squawked a reply, but Osler began shaking again and his thoughts drifted away from the staccato conversation between Sgt. Mallory and the Coast Guard. His throat tightened as he thought about home and his wife. *I don't want to die out here.*

He looked up when he heard Sgt. Mallory say his name, and was able to catch the reply from the speakers: "…the status on the shooting victim?"

"Need med-evac," said Sgt. Mallory. "Now."

"Copy. En route."

Sgt. Mallory turned to Osler. "Medical help's on the way. Now, where are my damn keys?"

❖

Valdez, Alaska

Chief Petty Officer Marcus Bolt slipped into the cabin of a 25-foot Defender-class US Coast Guard fast response boat. He donned his comm system, sat down in the front port seat and turned to the coxswain, Petty Officer First Class Odin Perry, who was busy finalizing the checklist and powering up the vessel.

"What's the mission?" he asked. "Another drill?"

"Orders are to intercept a vessel in Passage Canal," replied CPO1 Perry, "S&R's flying out to pick up a shooting victim at Whittier."

CPO Bolt reached for his tactical helmet, on the back of which someone (probably an officer) had stealthily stenciled *Lightning* – and was thrust backwards as Perry pushed the throttle forward and the dual 225-horsepower Honda outboard engines rocketed the vessel out to sea. He and Perry had been paired together for six months and had developed a trusting relationship, probably because they'd arrived in Valdez at about the same time and had been mercilessly picked on by the established Coasties. Someone (probably the same officer) had stenciled the name *Hazard* on the back of Perry's helmet, in a nod to the 1812-era naval commander, Oliver Hazard Perry. Bolt imagined that they had probably chortled and slapped each other on the back in the officers' mess about the name pairing on their assigned boat, Delta Four.

"Delta Four is outbound," said Perry, and punched data into the navigation system.

"Delta Two is outbound," crackled a voice in Bolt's headset.

"Any other info?" asked Bolt, strapping on his helmet. He looked out to port to see the orange-skirted, silver-grey hull of Delta Two catching up with them, and the base receding into the fog.

"CO was pissing himself. Some bad shit's happening."

Bolt studied the nav and radar systems, and then read the weather report. The fog would stay dense over the sound for several more hours but was clearing on land. He stopped to listen to orders coming through on his headset: the target vessel was running black, meaning the automated identification system was off; Delta Four and Delta Two were told to interdict but not board, because cutters and full support were on the way; and, most importantly, they were told to assume there was extreme radiation hazard on board, and to avoid firing on the vessel.

Bolt glanced at Perry to make sure he'd heard the same thing. He felt a sinking feeling gripping his guts. With his right hand, he reached for a spot in the center of his chest and pushed against his cold-suit and body armor until he felt metal scrape against his skin: the crucifix his wife had given him. He uttered a quick prayer and went through his own checklist as the boats turned south.

The dense fog forced Bolt's attention to flip between the radar screen and the view off the bow, as he scanned for hazards. Radar would pick up vessels but would miss small – but important – obstacles like logs, orcas, and kayakers. The fear of striking an object at their current speed of 35 knots – which might incapacitate the boat or even kill them both, not to mention the *striker* – helped temporarily distract from the part of the orders that referred to *extreme radiation hazard*.

Bolt knew the vessel they were pursuing had no chance of escaping. He looked at the icon on the screen, which was being relayed by the vessel tracking system radar array at Valdez. The target might escape detection by the Defender boats alone – were it behind one of the many islands in Prince William Sound, for example – but not the VTS.

"They're headed into Culross Passage. Five klicks," said Perry. He eased off the throttle and nodded at Bolt, which meant it was time to man the bow gun. Bolt got up from his seat, slid back the door, and stepped out into a gale of frigid air. He leaned forward against the wind with practiced foot placements over the bouncing deck, and attached himself to the 7.62 mm machine gun. Once secured, he gave a quick salute to Perrry, and then a thumbs up to Delta Two's gunner.

Standing behind the gun, on the bow of a small but very fast and nimble boat zipping and bouncing across the sea, struck Bolt's imagination in different ways, depending upon the roughness of the weather and waves. In the past he'd imagined himself standing with a long-handled axe behind the dragon's-head prow of a Viking raider; manning a ballista on the bow of a Greek trireme, hurtling flaming projectiles at Xerxes' fleet; or listening to punk music while surfing the Banzai Pipeline with an assault rifle.

Right now, he was spitless with fear.

"How the fuck did they find us?" screamed Raider-cap, staring at the two blips closing fast on the trawler's stern, only two kilometers away.

"Lad, the plans were for sleep and stealth; stealin' and sneakin' out," growled the captain. "You shot up the police, alarms went off – and then you shot up my damn ship." He rubbed the lump on his temple and peered through the fog.

"We gotta do something!"

"We can't outrun 'em. Gig's up, I think."

Raider-cap paced, and then flung open the hatch and stepped out to look astern. He couldn't see the boats but he could hear the engines echoing off the shores that bounded the narrow passage. Darting back into the wheelhouse. he said, "Got a surprise for them. Do exactly as I say or you're a dead man."

Despite the flashing blue lights and calls over the loudspeakers to halt, the trawler trudged on, apparently ignoring the two Defender boats flanking its stern. They had matched the vessel's 15 knots: fast for a fishing trawler, but to Bolt it felt like a leisurely cruise on a stand-up paddleboard. He couldn't see onto the deck or into the wheelhouse of the taller vessel because of the angle and the tall steel gunwales ringing the trawler. There were no crew anywhere to be seen. But *someone* was piloting it through the narrow channel, avoiding both the rocky outcrops extending from the shore and the shallows rising up from the bottom. Surely whoever was onboard must be aware of the Coast Guard yelling at them to heave to.

Bolt felt a tingling on the back of his neck. The fact that the trawler had no way to escape, yet refused to yield, usually suggested a skipper who was distracted, drunk, or panicked about a hold full of heroin. The latter circumstance sometimes lead to gun battles.

But this is a different scenario, he thought. *A different one altogether.*

He searched along the length of the vessel through the gun sights, alert for whatever might happen next. And then he thought again about the radiation hazard: *Are they planning on using that as a weapon? Are they beaming lethal rays at me right now?*

In the minutes that followed, Bolt listened to the comm chatter on his headset as he stared intently at the trawler: Perry discussed tactics with Delta Two, and the CO at Valdez weighed in. They decided to avoid confrontation but pace the trawler from bow and stern; one Defender leading and one following. So, one of the Defenders needed to get out front to shepherd and warn other ships away. At the southern end of the passage two USCG cutters would assist in halting the trawler.

Bolt watched Defender Two surge forward and disappear around the starboard side of the vessel. The trawler abruptly yawed to starboard, much faster than Bolt would have thought possible for a vessel of that size, and he had a clear view along the starboard side as it tried to pinch Delta Two against the rocks. Suddenly, men sprang from behind the gunwales and opened fire on Delta Two.

Fragments of glass, plastic and metal flew into the air as Delta Two powered into a 180-degree turn away from the gunfire and sped back.

"Taking fire!"

"Delta Two, Delta Four: you are cleared to engage threats, but watch the cargo."

Bolt felt the power transfer from the deck into his legs as Delta Four leapt forward to pass on the port side. He pivoted the gun to keep the sights on the trawler and was not surprised when it yawed towards him. His heart hammered as men popped up again and began firing.

He saw four muzzle flashes pulsing at him, and he depressed the trigger. Thwacks, cracks, and pings erupted around him as he squeezed off short bursts from the machine gun.

Shit. Shit. Shit!

The deck under Bolt's feet bounced with the surging acceleration, which made aiming tough; he swiveled the weapon, seeking flashes of light. Then he was punched in the chest, knocked backward and almost ripped from his safety harness. He gasped for air and knelt, hugging the gun-stand.

Through his headset he heard, "Bolt. Bolt!"

Delta Four sped several hundred yards ahead of the trawler, just out of visual range in the thinning fog, then cut the engines and spun about. Bolt recovered his breathing and stood. He gave a thumbs up to Odin and peered into the fog: a bow emerged, then more muzzle flashes. Bolt kept the trigger down as he guided the tracers to the bow and then back towards the wheelhouse.

He stopped firing.

About twenty heartbeats later, the trawler pitched and heaved, and then the bow wave settled.

As it coasted closer, Delta Four slid out of the way and Bolt swung the gun to cover the trawler as it slowed. He shook with adrenalin as he pivoted the gun back and forth, looking for threats, but then he saw men with raised hands.

"They're standing down. Hold fire!" he said into his mic.

"*Copy.*"

His headset announced the arrival of the cutters, and he glanced over to see the bows of two white ships with orange chevrons. They converged, deck guns aimed at the trawler.

Bolt kept his weapon ready, his right index-finger resting against the trigger guard. Seconds passed and nothing happened. He slipped his left hand to his chest to find a hole in his insulated over-suit; nausea gripped his guts. He used his teeth to remove his left glove and probed deeper into the hole with his fingertips. It continued through his body armor, and then his index finger felt intact skin. He exhaled sharply and placed his shaking left hand back on the gun.

Two rigid-inflatable boats motored over from the cutters, and ten Coasties boarded the trawler. Bolt listened to the audio feed as they secured the vessel, glanced at the damaged orange skirt of Delta Four, and then discovered the bullet holes and cracked glass in the cockpit.

"It's a little crunchy in here, but I'm good," said Odin.

Thirty bobbing minutes later, Bolt picked out his name from the comm chatter: "Chief Petty Officer Bolt. This is Lieutenant Jones. Come on board the trawler."

"Yes sir," Bolt answered into his mic.

Delta Four pulled alongside the trawler. Bolt's heart sank at the thought of what he might see as he climbed the rungs and stepped onto the deck. He hoped it wasn't a dead child or a dog.

He found the officer and saluted. Lt. Jones had a deeply furrowed brow and penetrating grey eyes, and was about a foot shorter than him, yet somehow he managed to tower above Bolt. The Coasties from the cutters had corralled the surviving trawler crew amidships. Bolt looked them over. Most stared at the deck or out at the water, but one of them, a linebacker-sized man with long red hair, briefly locked eyes with Bolt. He was sitting near the shot-up wreckage of a giant array of speakers. Bolt studied the damage. From his perspective as a gunner, they looked like they'd been shredded from the starboard side at close range. *Not me*, he thought.

Please, God, not kids or dogs.

"Good shooting, Chief Petty Officer Bolt," said the lieutenant. Then he stared at Bolt's uniform. "Are you injured?"

"Thank you, sir. No, sir, it didn't make it all the way through," Bolt replied woodenly. *Cut to the chase, sir. Why am I here, and not on my boat?*

"This whole affair is pretty damn strange, and I wanted you to see it," Lt. Jones said, and then gestured over his shoulder. "These speakers are part of an extensive sound system with generators, computer-controlled mix consoles, signal processors, and amplifiers – worthy of a Foo Fighters concert."

Lt. Jones studied Bolt with a penetrating look. "The skipper says he was just hired to run legal cargo. But the guy paying him went crazy, threatened the crew, shot up the speakers, and took over the trawler."

Bolt raised an eyebrow and opened his mouth, but the lieutenant wasn't finished.

"We're not exactly sure, but we have some intel that this sound system was somehow used to keep the folks in Whittier asleep, while the thieves here stole radioisotopes from a train – some kind of sound hypnosis." He shrugged. "Follow me to the hold."

As they walked past the wheelhouse, Bolt paused at the open hatch and looked inside. The forward windows were shot out and much of the navigation equipment and electronics – actually, way more stuff than should be on a

120-foot trawler – had been wrecked by Bolt's gunfire. As his eyes adjusted to the interior lights, he saw a scene like that of the slaughterhouse his father had dragged him to as a child, as part of his education in how the world worked. Blood covered almost the entire floor of the small space and was splattered on the aft wall. A corpse was bundled up in the corner, and a black Raiders hat rested on the blood-splattered deck.

"Four of the crew are dead, including this guy," said the lieutenant, next to Bolt's ear, startling him. "Two are injured. Total crew of twelve including the skipper. And one passenger: thirteen. We recovered a variety of military weapons including Kalashnikovs, ARs, and Uzis. Passenger's an old woman who tried to read fortunes for us. Said she was kidnapped." He chuckled.

Bolt followed the lieutenant to the hold and descended the narrow steps. It was brightly lit, and a Coastie was taking photographs while another took notes. A third moved around with what looked like a microphone on a thick wire that connected to a book-sized metal box with an LED screen. The Coastie with the box looked up and said, "No hot spots. Still only normal background radiation, sir."

The lieutenant nodded and pointed to three identical cubes, each about a meter across, in the center of the hold. "Take a look at those, Bolt."

Bolt could easily see the giant radiation warning symbols on each cube, but nevertheless he stepped closer: each looked heavy and appeared to have been designed so that the top third of the cube could be removed – once the eight locking hasps had been disengaged. He looked at the less familiar labels. One was a red triangle with a black border and black icons: a skull and crossbones in the bottom left; a radiation trefoil in the apex, with five wiggly arrow-tips beaming down like rays from the sun; and, at the bottom-right, a stick figure running after an arrow pointing to one side. Bolt had seen this warning sign in training years ago. It meant extremely lethal radiation.

"Type B radiation packaging, sir?" he asked.

"Aye."

Bolt looked at another label: *Cs-137*.

Christ!

"Cesium-137, sir," he said. "That's the really nasty one, like in the exclusion zone around Chernobyl."

"Yes. And it will be around that melted reactor for a hundred years or more."

"What's cesium doing here, sir?" asked Bolt.

"The crew here hijacked a medical shipment, I think. We'll know more when the numbers on these containers are run. Transportation of nuclear materials is kept secret, so they must've had inside information," said the lieutenant. The intense stare – which had Bolt continuously on edge – softened. "There'll be a lot of questions coming up as this is investigated, but I wanted to show you how important this interdiction was."

"Yes, sir."

"Good job today. Now please get back to base and clean up. CO wants to see you."

Osler watched the 6 pm news coverage from within a post-general-anesthesia haze in his hospital room in Anchorage. It gave him a curious blend of déjà vu, anxiety, and detachment. He was still struggling with the thought that it was all real and that he had actually been involved.

Earlier, right after he got out of the post-anesthesia care unit and was taken to his room, he had called his wife. He had downplayed the injury, and the repair that the vascular surgeon had performed: *He said it wasn't a big deal to fix that artery, dear. I'm fine. Really.*

He knew she was right to be upset with him. He even tried the *Hey – look, honey, I stopped the bad terrorists* excuse, but got no traction. Anne cried, and that made him feel like a jerk for risking his life. He promised her he would stick to neurology, with occasional forays into the yard to cut the grass or pick a daisy, for the foreseeable future.

The news was showing aerial video footage of the trawler being tug-boated into dock in Anchorage and reporting that authorities had recovered stolen cesium-137 from the vessel. The news anchor hypothesized that the crime might have been headed by a terrorist group intent on making a dirty bomb. "Authorities haven't released any further details, but we'll continue to provide updates as they come in…"

Osler felt sick as the shock of the words 'cesium-137' settled into his mind. *My God!*

His hospital room door swung slowly inwards and someone stepped in. Osler focused to see Kalliope carrying a shoulder bag. Her brows were drawn down, and as she stepped closer, he watched her eyes flick over the IV pole – with its clear plastic bag of saline and its boxy infusion pump – and then fix on the suction drain hanging from the bed. Her blue and brown eyes traced the length of red-fluid-filled plastic tubing up to the point where it disappeared under the white bandages around his thigh.

Osler smiled and signed excitedly, "Hello. It's great to see you."

He thought that the morphine must have made him slur the words, botching the correct hand positions, because there was no immediate reaction from Kalliope. But as she stepped closer, Osler saw the expression of concern on her face relax and eyebrows raise. Her chin trembled as she signed, "I was so worried."

He smiled, trying to hide the pain, and signed, "You're very thoughtful. I'm doing great."

Kalliope brushed a long white forelock away from her face, searching his eyes. Osler sensed that she wasn't buying it.

"Really. I'm OK," he signed. "I'll be out tomorrow."

She nodded and held out his messenger bag. "The rest of your luggage is on a cart in the hallway. Walt returned your rental car."

"Thank you," he signed. "What time did the tunnel open?"

"Noon," she signed, and then bit her lip and paused before continuing. "How's your leg?"

"Let me show you," he signed. He fished his laptop and a notepad out of the bag, then reached over to the bedside stand for the DVD containing his MRI angiogram. He maneuvered the rolling tray-table, opened his laptop, and slotted in the disc. After a moment, a window appeared with a single greyscale image, bordered by a matrix of smaller images. The main image was a cross-section of his right thigh, like a slice taken through the trunk of a tree. By hitting the left and right arrow keys, Osler could cycle through the thin sections.

Osler wrote *MRI angiogram* on the notepad. Kalliope motioned for the pen and wrote *gadolinium* underneath. Osler smiled and signed, "Yes. How did you know?"

Kalliope wrote *comparative biology class – we used MRI images to help learn anatomy.*

"Excellent," signed Osler.

She then wrote, *They did this to see if an artery was leaking, right?*

Osler nodded.

Kalliope motioned for the laptop and he spun it so she could use the keyboard whilst allowing them both to see the screen. He watched her cycle through the images: the brightest white area in each picture was the gadolinium within the arterial system. She went through the entire sequence and then came back to two images, then flicked back and forth between them. She pointed to a fuzzy white zone outside the cross-sectional white circle of the artery.

"Here," she signed.

"Yes!" signed Osler. He wrote out: *Small tear in a minor branch off the femoral artery. They put a few micro-sutures in to repair it. I'll need some rest and then physical therapy for the damaged muscles but should be back to work in two weeks. I'm lucky.*

The whole town thanks you, she wrote. *You saved us.*

Thank you for setting off the tsunami warning and saving my life.

Kalliope smiled and wrote, *We're a good team!* Then her eyebrows shot up and she added, *My mom wanted me to tell you that she found the cowboys passed out in the snow, next to an empty tequila bottle, and covered with frozen vomit.*

Awesome, wrote Osler. Then he took out a business card and wrote his personal email address on it. He flipped it over to write a message and handed the card to Kalliope. She looked at the front and then turned it over to read to message: *Kalliope, pursue your dream to become a physician. You have the critical three ingredients: empathy, intelligence, and equanimity.*

"Please stay in touch. You are an amazing individual, and I am happy to help you in your career," he signed.

Kalliope beamed and signed, "Thank you. I will."

ABOUT THE AUTHOR

MARK JENKINS

Mark's insatiable curiosity has driven him to biochemistry, college-athletics, medical school, triathlon, internal medicine, teaching, Ironman races, writing, skydiving, motorcycling, martial arts, and mountain climbing.

Some of his favorite fiction authors are J.R.R. Tolkien, Neal Stephenson, Tom Clancy, Stephen King, Dean Koontz, William Gibson, and Dan Simmons.

Mark is an avid cyclist and a lover of salmon. He currently lives in the Pacific Northwest where he and his wife, Jo, enjoy hiking, climbing, stand-up paddle boarding (when Mark can stay upright), photography, and quiet walks in nature.

—

Thank you for reading **Klickitat— and other stories.**

Now that you have finished, I would love if you could take a moment to leave a review on the site where you purchased the book, and/or on Goodreads

---

Want to keep up with what's fun and happening in my writing world? Please visit **MarkJenkinsbooks.com** and sign up for my periodic newsletter.

And as a final thought, some secrets are best shared, so please feel free to spread the word about *Klickitat* to family and friends, and on social media.

Happy Adventures,
Mark

This page intentionally left blank

Printed in Great Britain
by Amazon

54395418R00113